With Love,
Selina 2014

**Heavenly Realm Publishing Company**
*Houston, Texas*

# CROWNED
# AT THE CROSS

# GELINA GILBERT

ISBN—13-  978-0-9825589-1-1
ISBN—10-  0-9825589-1-1

Library of Congress Control Number:  2009942064

This book is printed on acid free paper.

Printed in the United States of America

Unless otherwise indicated, all scriptures quotations in this book are from the King James Version of the Holy Bible.

*Published By:* **Heavenly Realm Publishing,**
**505 N. Sam Houston Parkway E., Suite 670,**
**Houston, Texas 77060,**
**local: 1-281-999-3237, toll free: 1-877-599-3237.**

# CONTENTS

# IN LOVING MEMORY

I dedicate this story to my great-grandmother, Manon Carrie Edwards, who was born in Hunt County, Texas on March 29, 1912. She lived a dedicated life, serving the Lord. She passed away on March 4, 2009 at almost 97-years-old, leaving behind one son, four daughters, numerous grandchildren, great-grandchildren, and great-great-grandchildren.

I know that a crown of life awaits her.

# ACKNOWLEDGEMENTS

I want to thank all of my family and friends. You all have been such a great support, not just in my writing, but in my life. I could never thank you all enough.

Special thanks to Grandma Rita. Words cannot describe my appreciation to you. You're a wonderful spiritual and natural mentor. You're also a great friend.

Lastly, I want thank the martyrs who gave up their lives for the cause of Jesus Christ. Because of their willing sacrifices, we have courage to stand for the Lord when our faith is challenged. I respect them for their valiant surrender.

Today, the world needs such strong leaders of faith as they were then.

# CROWNED AT THE CROSS

GELINA GILBERT

# CHAPTER ONE

*The Death of a Friend*
*Italy, 250 A.D.*

Stephen's heart raced as he grabbed his knife. He and ten-year-old Fabian ran into the woods. The horses of Roman soldiers broke the silence of the wintry night.

"God, save us!" He breathed a sincere prayer, "Please let us return to our family!"

"Halt in the name of Rome!" was a boisterous shout from behind them. It echoed through the trees, seeming to penetrate the core of Stephen's heart.

Fabian stumbled. Stephen struggled to help him stand.

"Don't stop," Stephen warned him, panting. Several more shouts were hurled from behind.

When Fabian couldn't run any longer, Stephen grabbed him up into his arms. Stephen felt his legs begin to weaken. He collapsed in fatigue.

"They'll kill us!" Fabian cried, jumping to his feet.

"Go, Fabian, now!" Stephen shouted at him. Fabian searched his brother-in-law's tired face.

He shook his head defiantly and looked through the woods as the soldiers approached them with lighted torches.

Fabian began to weep. "C'mon, Stephen!" he whined. He grabbed Stephen's shirt sleeve, and it tore away in his hand. Stephen gripped Fabian's wrist and managed to stand.

Roman soldiers surrounded them. A soldier slipped from his horse and approached them. "Are you two citizens of Rome?"

"We are," Stephen answered.

"Then you ought to halt when it is commanded of you in the name of Rome." The soldier studied them. "Who are you? Tell us your names," he demanded.

"I'm Stephen Galagus, and this is my brother-in-law, Fabian Mauritius."

"What is the purpose of your roaming this country? Are you Christians?" Fabian looked to Stephen as he trembled in fear.

"We were hunting in these woods for food," said Stephen. Then he tossed his knife into the snow. "Yes, I do believe in Jesus Christ."

"Do you have a Certificate of Sacrifice for worshiping the Roman observance?"

"No," Stephen said. "We have not and will not sacrifice to your gods."

The solider raised an eyebrow at him. "If you refuse to obey our emperor's command and swear your allegiance, I have the right to arrest you and have you put to death."

Stephen nodded. "I know." He grabbed Fabian's arm and turned to the soldiers in desperation. "But I beg you, if you arrest me, please spare this boy!"

"We're already loaded with prisoners," another armed man told the soldier. "Leave the boy. He'll more than likely freeze tonight anyway."

The Roman soldier nodded. "So shall it be done." Two soldiers dismounted and shoved Fabian away from Stephen. Grabbing Stephen by his broad shoulders, the soldiers began to beat him with force.

"Stephen!" Fabian screamed as tears rolled down his face.

"Run!" Stephen yelled back to Fabian. He was gagged soon afterward.

Fabian ran until he knew he could no longer be seen. He turned and looked back, unable to leave. He watched Stephen slip from consciousness.

"Let's not bother to take him back to the wagon," Fabian heard one soldier say. "Just be done with him." Fabian turned away in agony as a Roman soldier drew his sword.

2

Stumbling through the woods, Fabian tripped and fell into the snow. He weakly rose to his feet, pushing away brown wisps of hair that clung to his forehead. Visions of Stephen flooded his mind. He tried to forget the last look he saw in his friend's eyes. His mind reeled with what he would tell his sister and his parents.

*This is what we've feared since we left Rome last year*, he thought with dread.

Fabian hurried through the small entrance of their underground living quarters, which was nestled in the hidden shadows of a ravine. He scampered through the stair-like tunnel, pushing his way past the twigs and branches used to conceal the passageway.

He entered the dimly-lit room. A small fire burned. A hole above the fire had been chopped in the ground to draw the smoke from the room. Everyone was sleeping, huddled around the fire, clinging to one another for warmth.

Fabian wiped away his tears, searching for his sister. Carefully stepping over his parents, he found his twenty-year-old sister, Lavenya, sleeping with her four-year-old daughter, Julia. He knelt beside them and shook his sister's shoulder.

"Lavenya," he whispered, "Lavenya!"

Her eyelids fluttered open as she awoke. The light from the fire revealed his tears. She sat up with a start, gripping Fabian's hand.

"Did something go wrong in the hunt?"

"It's Stephen," he said, trying to catch his breath. "Soldiers followed our trail. They questioned us about being Christians. Stephen told them we were." His voice quivered, "They let me go, but they grabbed Stephen and beat him. Then . . . they . . . ."

Lavenya leaned forward earnestly as he said, "Lavenya, Stephen is dead."

# CHAPTER TWO

*The Oath of Commission*

A handsome, young man in his late twenties sat in the veranda of a fine, Roman villa. His gaze lingered over the skyline of the city. He leapt forward, hearing the large, wooden doors open and close with a deafening slam.

His elderly mother came limping toward him as she cried, "Your brother was killed! I just got word from my servant!"

Julian listened in disbelief as his mother spoke. The tears that formed in her eyes and the way she shook in complete distraught, seemed to tell him it was true. He drew her into a strong embrace. "Don't despair, Mother," he comforted. "Stephen was influenced by those rebels."

"I lost my youngest son."

Julian sucked in a deep breath. "You won't lose me." He sat down beside her on a bench near a springing fountain.

"Your illness will worsen if you afflict yourself with misery. We knew this would happen when he joined those madmen. They are completely fanatical."

"They've converted thousands," his elderly mother said. "They must be stopped."

She gripped her chest in pain and groaned. Julian caught her arm. He yelled for a servant. He dictated orders to get a physician. The servant hurried into their large estate.

She gripped his hand. "Julian," she cried hoarsely, "they must be stopped."

"Mother!" Julian yelled in pain as he saw his mother's eyes turn away from him, and life slip away from her. He pulled her lifeless form into his arms and wept. "Mother!"

Julian felt someone shake him awake. His servant stood above him. He blinked sleep from his eyes and sat up gruffly.

"What's the meaning of this?" he demanded, wiping a hand through his black hair.

"Valerian is at the door. He wants to see you."

"Let him in," Julian said in a groggy mumble.

Valerian came into the room with a half smile. He nodded to his friend, shaking his hand. He scooted a chair to his bedside and sat down. "You must be feeling better."

"As best as I can be, seeing my mother and brother are dead."

"How long has it been since you last saw Stephen?" Valerian asked.

Julian sighed. "Six years. Mother and I didn't have anything to do with him after he betrayed our gods. If Father were alive, he would have killed him."

Valerian shook his head. "Well, I have something that might ease your pain, my friend." He held up two tickets. "I purchased these myself. These are seats near Emperor Decius himself. We'll have a clear view of the arena; there are executions announced for this afternoon."

Julian grinned and sat up. "It'd make me feel good to see those fools eaten."

"Oh, it isn't a lion hunt." Valerian chuckled. "It's a burning."

"The more Christians I see roasted, the better," Julian said with a cruel laugh. "They're the reason my brother and mother are dead. Now, I'm alone in this terrible world."

"You have a fine home with the most exquisite, warm baths and furnishings—what more could you want?" Valerian asked with a chuckle, hoping to cheer his friend.

"A visit to the Colosseum," Julian said, yanking the tickets from him.

Julian and Valerian were seated in the tenth row from the emperor's grandstand, where he was surrounded by adoring citizens. The Colosseum was thronged with shouting Roman citizens. Julian studied the people around him, seeing several wealthy noblemen and women, making their way to the lower seats.

The view lightened his heart, just as Valerian had told him it would. Julian leaned back in his seat as Valerian elbowed him, pointing to the cage being opened in the arena.

"They're bringing out the Christians," he said. Julian leaned forward to study the simply dressed people being led into the arena, met by shouts and whistles from the horde of people in the stands. There were eight Christians—two of them were children.

Julian saw the frightened look in their eyes as the soldiers led them to their crosses. Anger boiled inside him as he clenched his fist.

"That's what you deserve!" he shouted, but his voice faded with the roaring crowd. Valerian and Julian were on their feet, shouting and cheering along with the crowd as the torches were lit. They waited as the soldiers set fire to the crosses. Julian frowned, not hearing the Christians cry out. He looked to Valerian as they waited to hear groans of pain. Julian looked closer and nudged Valerian.

"Those crazed fools . . . are singing!" he said in disbelief.

The crowd watched with cheers as the crosses blazed with fire. Julian shook his head, unable to believe that the Christians were singing, despite their torture. "They're singing in some kind of . . . language. Those people must be devilish. It's probably a curse they're trying to sing on us!" Julian told Valerian.

The crowd took their seats to watch the burning with amusement and laughter. Julian chuckled as he saw soldiers teasing each other in the middle of the arena.

After Valerian had been quiet for some time, Julian felt a tug on his arm.

"Did you see that?" his friend asked with alarm.

"See what?" Julian demanded, being roused from his comfort.

Valerian slowly stood to his feet and pointed. "There was an angel in the arena!"

"You must be out of your mind." Julian stood with embarrassment to urge his friend back to his seat. Julian saw several Romans staring at them with amusement. "Don't you see you're making a fool of yourself in front of all these people?"

"It *was* an angel," Valerian repeated dazedly. He turned to Julian with tears in his eyes. He shook his head persistently and bolted from his seat. "Julian, their god is real!"

Julian watched in horror as Valerian headed down the stairs. He hurried after him, yelling at him to stop. Julian caught up with him and tried to grab his arm, but Valerian jumped from the balcony, landing on the floor of the arena.

"Valerian!" Julian shouted, not believing what he saw.

The crowd let out a surprised yell as Valerian ran toward a soldier who was standing beside one of the blazing stakes. Valerian drew his sword, but the soldier turned too quickly.

The soldier thrust his sword forward, killing him.

"Valerian!" Julian yelled in disbelief as the soldier grabbed Valerian, and threw his limp body into the flames.

Julian walked dazedly through the streets of Rome as he left the arena, feeling pain grip his heart. *Why had Valerian been so foolish?*

Walking through the marketplace, Julian stopped at hearing a muffled voice. Turning, he caught sight of an elderly man clutching a cross, praying.

"Away with your devilish prayers!" Julian yelled at the man before he could stop himself—what he had witnessed in the arena was too great. He felt tears welling up in his eyes.

He hurried to the man, grabbed the cross from him, and threw it on the ground. The elderly man grunted in surprise and bent to pick up the cross.

"No! It isn't devilish," the man gasped, clutching the cross to his chest.

"I should have you killed!" Julian yelled and sent the man a curled punch. The man staggered and fell back onto the ground, bleeding from a deep head wound.

"Halt in the name of Rome!"

Julian felt a firm hand on his shoulder. He turned, meeting the rigid face of a young soldier. Then the soldier looked to each of them. Julian stood with his fists clenched. The man gripped at his bleeding forehead in agony.

"What's the meaning of this?" the soldier asked.

"This man is a Christian," Julian said.

The soldier turned to the man. "Do you have a Certificate of Sacrifice?"

"No, sir." The elderly man tried to catch his breath.

"Then you shall be arrested." The soldier nodded to another soldier who stood beside him. He immediately grabbed the man, jerking him to his feet. Julian clenched his bloody fist as the man was dragged away, groaning in pain.

"He won't last, I can assure you," the soldier told Julian.

Julian tightened his jaw. "Good."

"I must admit, I am impressed by your allegiance to our emperor. Who are you?"

"Julian Galagus. And I do worship and sacrifice to our gods."

The soldier nodded. "I see. My name is Caspian Pertinius." The soldier leaned closer to him, lowering his voice, "Tonight I'll send for you, Julian. I'll have a horse ready for you. You'll be brought to our fortification just outside the city."

"What is the meaning of this summons?" Julian asked him with a frown.

"The centurion shall give you an assignment. I sense you are the man he is looking for. You must obey your emperor, Julian," the soldier said. Then he was gone.

Julian followed the horseman in front of him, holding the reins to his own brown stallion. Questions lurked in his mind as he followed the soldier through the city gates, where the Roman fortified garrison was established.

The soldier and Julian halted their horses just beyond the entrance and dismounted.

"The centurion demands your presence," the soldier told him.

Caspian greeted him with a respectable nod and led him inside a large tent, where several important men were sitting around a lavishly prepared table.

"Prostrate yourself before him," Caspian hissed to Julian, immediately kneeling down. Julian quickly followed.

"Rise!" the centurion barked. Julian jumped to his feet. The centurion turned to his officers and then to Caspian. "A stocky, young man, isn't he?" He chuckled along with the other men. "We should have made him a soldier."

"We may be able convince him to join the legion as time goes on," Caspian said.

Julian studied them. *'As time goes on'? What will they ask of me?*

"Caspian says you have a Certificate of Sacrifice?" the centurion asked. "You honor the gods of Rome and no other?"

Julian looked up at them with a firm nod. "I serve the gods of my father gladly and I am *not* a Christian," he said with distaste.

"You seem fervent in that." The centurion raised his eyebrows with a chuckle to the men beside him.

Julian nodded, remembering his brother and mother. And there was Valerian. "I believe all Christians should be exterminated."

"Then you are perfect for the work, which I shall commission you." The centurion nodded resolutely. Julian frowned and studied them as a scribe began to write on a scroll.

"What is this commission? I'm simply a Roman, taking up my father's trade."

"We are looking for such men as you," the centurion told him. "We are looking for men who are zealous enough to inform us of the locations of Christians. We know they're hiding out in the hills. We want them found and brought back, prisoners to Rome."

"Why haven't the soldiers been assigned this task?" Julian asked.

"We need every able-bodied soldier to protect our city from barbarian invasion. Your work will not be with the sword, but with diplomacy." The centurion nodded to him. "You shall be informed of what you need to do. Then you will search for Christian locations, so we can send our soldiers to arrest them. You'll be rewarded handsomely."

"I will do this task with all of my strength," Julian told them. "Christianity must end."

The centurion took the scroll from the scribe, placing his own seal upon it. He stood. Julian knelt to the ground. "Make an oath to remain truthful and obedient to the Roman Empire and our gods. You shall find locations of Christian radicals," the centurion dictated.

"I will fight and die under this oath," Julian vowed.

"Good." The centurion ordered him to his feet.

Julian stood. A servant handed him the scroll.

"You shall present this to anyone who tries to prevent you, and if they persist, you have the authority to destroy them," the centurion instructed and nodded to Caspian. "Now then, Caspian shall give you further instruction."

# CHAPTER THREE

## A Victorious God

"If the Romans know about Stephen, we must proceed carefully."

Lavenya listened to her father as they were gathered around the fire. "They may come back to search this area. If they find us here, we will be arrested and executed.

"If we do not honor the pagan gods, Emperor Decius will act upon us with vengeance. Though many have compromised, we must remain true to the Lord."

Lavenya coddled her daughter in her arms as tears spilled down her cheeks. *Lord, how long will these persecutions last?* she prayed. *Will we have to live like this until the end of our days? Will Julia have to grow up here—unable to marry and have children?*

Her daughter pulled back from her and placed her hand on Lavenya's cold cheek. Dimples entered her pink cheeks as she said, "Don't cry, Mama."

"I will try not to, dear." Lavenya pulled her daughter into her arms and cried.

"We must pray to the Lord; only God can save us," Stantius Mauritius said, looking to his daughter and his granddaughter with sorrowful eyes. "We'll miss Stephen, but we can be thankful in knowing he is in the hands of God."

Lavenya wiped tears from her eyes as her father picked up a scroll. He opened it slowly, studying the words.

He began to read, "Paul told us these encouraging words, "*Who shall separate us from the love of Christ? shall tribulation, or distress, or persecution, or famine, or nakedness, or peril, or sword?*

*"As it is written, For thy sake we are killed all the day long;
we are accounted as sheep for the slaughter.*

*"Nay, in all these things we are more than conquerors
through him that loved us.*

*"For I am persuaded, that neither death, nor life, nor angels,
nor principalities, nor powers, nor things present, nor things to
come,*

*"Nor height, nor depth, nor any other creature, shall be able
to separate us from the love of God, which is in Christ Jesus our
Lord."*

Stantius set the scroll on his lap with tears in his eyes. "We
have that same assurance today. Nothing can separate us from our
Lord; nothing has separated Stephen from the Lord. We can be
comforted in knowing that God will take care of his soul."

Lavenya moved Julia's brown curls between her fingers,
thinking of her husband. She felt peace soothe her heart as she
thought about her father's words.

She watched the others around the room as they embraced.
There was her mother, Martina, with Fabian and her older brother
and his wife, Lawrence and Cecilia. Cecilia's mother had caught
fever and died when she was a child. Her father disowned her after
learning of her faith in God.

There were other Christian families with them—an elderly
man and his wife, Rufus and Lydia. Lawrence had rescued them
before they were killed. They had lost their three children to the
swords of the merciless Romans.

A middle-aged man, Apuleius, sat with his wife, Alluvia.
Their ten-year-old daughter, Felicia, and teen-aged son, Titus, were
beside them comforting each other.

The last of the Christians were friends of Apuleius—Antony
and his young son, Claudius. His wife had been captured the
previous year and killed in the Colosseum.

*We've all had our share of pain,* Lavenya thought as she
watched them quietly praying. *We have had our share of burdens,
but we've had God's grace through it all. We can sing praises to our
Lord—we are still alive.*

Lavenya placed more wood on the fire while Cecilia gathered the cooking utensils to prepare what little food they had. She shivered in her coat, listening to Julia hum as she played with her dolls on their blankets.

Cecilia smiled as she worked. "It's good to have Julia here. She gives a bright smile in these times," Cecilia whispered. They lifted a large pot onto the fire to roast their dinner.

Lavenya smiled weakly. "I hope I can learn from her."

"You must be strong." Cecilia gave Lavenya a comforting smile. "I try to always encourage myself when I'm down. I always find comfort in God's love."

"Maybe you're the one who should uplift me then," Lavenya replied.

"We have much to be thankful for," Cecilia said. "We're alive and we're all together. We have gained encouragement from God's Word. It has shown us, just as your father read—nothing can separate us from God's love, not even death. We've had to give up so much, but Jesus gave so much more for us. Even our greatest sacrifice can never pay the debt we owe Him."

Lavenya thought negatively about her words. "Yes, we had to leave so much behind." She remembered leaving their fine estate in Rome and fleeing to the hills. They had left everything. *Everything but our faith—the most important thing of all.*

She was pulled from her thoughts when Cecilia coughed, placing a hand to her chest. Lavenya took her arm as she coughed uncontrollably.

"Are you okay?" Lavenya asked with concern.

Cecilia nodded, but coughed again. "I'm fine." The coughing faded.

Lavenya felt concerned. "You'd better rest while I finish the meal."

"I don't want to leave you with this burden," Cecilia protested.

"I'll be fine," Lavenya assured her. "Mother will assist me. I'll have our meal ready for everyone shortly. I'll wake you when it's finished."

Lavenya continued to stir the meat over the open fire. She turned, seeing her father and Fabian enter the passageway, looking disheartened.

"We were unable to find Stephen's body to have a proper burial," her father told her. She saw distress in his eyes, and knew it pained him to tell her.

Lavenya nodded and thought grimly, *The wild animals must have gotten him.* She turned away as tears formed in her eyes.

Stantius put an arm around her, placing his cheek to her forehead as he had done when she was a child. Lavenya wiped away her tears as he embraced her, releasing a sigh.

"God will be victorious," he whispered. "Remember, Lavenya, no matter how hard things may seem . . . God will have the ultimate victory."

"Thank you, Father."

"Mama, look at my dolly!"

Lavenya slipped from her father's grasp when she felt Julia tug on her long skirt. She pulled her daughter close.

"I see it. She's pretty like you." Lavenya kissed Julia's cheek. When she pulled back from her, she saw Julia frown as she studied her face.

"Mama, you been crying again," Julia accused.

Cecilia's words came back to Lavenya—"*You must be strong.*"

Before Lavenya could reply, Lawrence came hurrying inside the room, carrying several dead rabbits over his shoulder. Fabian grinned, hurrying to examine them.

"I hope this will keep us from having to go hunting, at least for a few more days," Lawrence told them, setting down his catch. He grinned up at them. "Food smells wonderful."

"It's almost ready," Lavenya said, setting Julia down.

She watched Lawrence walk toward Cecilia as she slept beneath several blankets. He knelt beside her, caressing her forehead with a worn hand.

"Her skin is very warm," Lawrence said with alarm. "I hope she isn't ill."

He gently stroked her forehead. The loving scene between

16

her brother and Cecilia reminded Lavenya of Stephen—she turned away.

She sighed and thought, *I don't want Julia to accuse me of crying again.*

# CHAPTER FOUR

## *A Night of Prayer*

Lavenya awoke, hearing someone stir in the night. Their fire still had a few sparking embers, so she hurried to add more wood to the fire. Hearing the movement again, she walked through the darkness, seeing Cecilia toss and turn beneath her blankets, groaning.

"Cecilia," Lavenya whispered, "Are you all right?"

"My stomach . . . it's in terrible pain."

Lavenya frowned, hearing her friend's weary voice. She knelt down beside her, taking her hand. "May I do something for you?"

"Please, wake Lawrence."

Lavenya found her brother sleeping beside her. She shook him, watching his face in the flickering firelight as he awoke. His eyes narrowed on her.

"Cecilia is in pain. She needs you."

At hearing her words, Lawrence turned to his wife's side and took her hand. "Cecilia?" he questioned with concern. "What's ailing you?"

"My stomach," she said with a groan and coughed.

"Get her some water," he told Lavenya. She hurried to pour water from what they had drawn from the river. Handing the decanter to him, Lawrence gave Cecilia a long drink.

They waited as she tossed beneath her blankets, seeming to slip in and out of sleep. Slowly Cecilia drifted to sleep.

Lawrence turned to his sister with concern. "She is terribly ill," he whispered.

"What must we do?" Lavenya asked, studying her friend's pale face.

"I'll travel tomorrow night to find a physician among the Christians. There's bound to be one hiding in this terrain with the rest of us," Lawrence said hopefully.

Lavenya felt doubtful, but wouldn't have expressed her thoughts aloud. When her brother didn't speak for some time, she turned to look at him and saw that his eyes were closed in prayer.

"Yes, we must pray for her continually," Lavenya whispered to him. He nodded and she saw tears drip down his face. He took Cecilia's hand and placed it to his lips, praying.

She took Cecilia's other hand and sat beside her all night in prayer.

"When I find a physician, I will return to you," Lawrence told the others as they sat to eat dinner that next evening.

Lavenya turned to Cecilia who was in a restless sleep beneath her blankets—she wasn't strong enough to eat.

"Our prayers will be with you until you return," her father told him.

"But think of the danger of traveling," Rufus said aloud. "With Romans scattered around these hills, you may not return, Lawrence."

"By the grace of God, I will." Lawrence looked to his restless wife. "I must."

"Why don't you take someone with you?" Stantius suggested.

"I'll go," Fabian offered, but Martina shook her head at him, causing him to pout.

"Apuleius has a wife and two children to look after," Antony spoke up. "I'll accompany you if the others take care of Claudius."

"I'd be thankful to have you come," Lawrence said. "It would be good if I had someone with me for defense purposes—two are better than one."

"Antony and I will watch your son," Stantius assured him, rubbing his hand through Claudius' hair with a grin.

"The sooner we start, the sooner she'll get well," Lawrence

said, standing to his feet.

He and Antony began to gather their things. Lydia and Martina hurried to get food for them. They thanked the women as they placed the food in their bags.

"We will return soon. We'll only travel at night," Lawrence said, putting on his coat. He then gave Stantius a hearty embrace.

"May God go with you and protect you, son," Stantius said, giving him a firm pat.

Lavenya turned away. Her father had said those same words to Stephen and Fabian when they'd gone hunting. She felt her heart tense inside her. *I must be strong,* she reminded herself.

She turned, hearing Cecilia groan. Not wanting to worry Lawrence and Antony further, she hurried to quiet her with a drink of water.

Lawrence hurried to his wife's side. "We will return with help, I promise," he whispered to her. He knelt down and stroked her cheek. "We will not return unless we find help for you." He leaned and gave her cold cheek a loving kiss.

Lavenya stayed by Cecilia's side as they left. She gave her more water to drink as her trembling body fidgeted beneath the blankets.

*Cecilia, you told me I must be strong for Julia,* Lavenya thought and gently stroked her friend's cheek. *Now, I must be strong for you.*

The frigid wind pressed hard against them as Lavenya and Martina gathered frozen bits of food from snowdrifts. The darkness of the night evaded them. The moon sparkled along the riverbank's chilly waters, giving them faint light.

Apuleius and Stantius were not far from them, chopping more wood for their fire. Fabian, Claudius, and Titus were there to assist them, stacking the wood in small piles.

"Is Julia inside?" Lavenya's mother asked her as she dug through the snow.

"Yes, Lydia and Felicia are with her. I'm so thankful Felicia is young enough to be a companion to her. I would hate for her to be raised with all boys."

"Cecilia is losing strength," Martina said in a low whisper.

"I know. It's been three days. If Lawrence doesn't return soon—I fear for her life." Lavenya turned to look at the darkened passageway to their home.

"I can't even think about losing another person I love," Lavenya said.

"With faith in Jesus, we won't lose anyone," Martina encouraged her. "With this bloody persecutor as our ruler, it may be the best thing for her."

"We must pray," was Lavenya's determined answer.

"Yes, and we can, but we also must believe that God will do what He wills," Martina reminded her, placing bits of roots in the small basket they were carrying.

Hearing the sound of horses in the distance, Lavenya gripped her mother's arm. "Do you hear that?" Then she fell silent, turning to look at the others.

Her father and the other men were poised, listening for the sound.

"Soldiers!" Martina whispered with dread.

They immediately dropped their baskets, causing the food they'd gathered to tumble to the ground. The boys dropped the wood from their arms and frantically rushed to the entrance of their home. Apuleius and Stantius shoved the boys in behind the women and then darted in themselves. They waited, embracing each other for comfort. Lavenya held Julia tightly.

A few seconds passed and they heard thundering horses' hooves shaking the ground above them, sending a cascade of rocks down on them. They listened to indistinct voices.

"Dear God," Stantius prayed aloud.

After several quiet minutes, the sound of the horses faded into the distance.

"She isn't getting stronger."

Lavenya listened to her mother and Lydia talking with Alluvia as they were sewing. Lavenya rocked Julia in her arms, trying to get her to sleep. She turned toward Cecilia who lay listlessly under her blankets.

"I wonder what is keeping Lawrence and Antony," Alluvia said.

"Maybe they can't find a doctor," Lydia said. "Lawrence said he wouldn't return unless they found someone to help her."

"They must return some time," Martina told them, sewing steadily. "My son is a headstrong, young man, but if he cannot find one, he will return to his wife."

"A few more days," Alluvia said and lowered her voice, "and he won't have a wife to return to."

Lavenya turned away, despising their words. She longed for Cecilia's recovery. Facing the death of her dear friend was not something she wanted to think about.

Seeing Julia had fallen asleep, she placed her daughter in her bedding and went to Cecilia's side. She reached for Cecilia's hand, and gave it a warm squeeze.

"You will get better, dearest," she whispered to her. "You must."

"Lavenya?" Cecilia slowly opened her eyes and coughed. Lavenya's hope increased.

She clasped her friend's hand with a hopeful smile. "Yes, it's me."

"Where is Lawrence?" Cecilia asked with another cough as her eyes searched the room. Her voice sounded terrible, causing Lavenya's heart to ache.

"He left two weeks ago." Lavenya then said, "He left to find help for you."

"No." Cecilia began to sit up, but Lavenya prevented her. The ladies came to Lavenya's side, seeing Cecilia stir in her blankets.

"Lawrence is going to find someone to help you," Lavenya comforted her. "Antony left with my brother to find a physician among the Christians."

"He'll be captured." Cecilia's eyes widened with fear. "I must get him."

When she started to sit up again, Lavenya prevented her by gently grabbing her by her shoulders. "You can't—he already left. Lie back down and try to rest," Lavenya told her. Cecilia protested, but her weary eyes slowly drifted shut as she lay back down.

"Dear Lord, have mercy on our poor girl," Lydia prayed with distress as Cecilia slipped into a deep sleep.

Lavenya's mother placed a hand on her shoulder, giving her a comforting squeeze.

"Lavenya! Lavenya!" She felt someone shaking her awake before dawn. Opening her eyes, she met her mother's tear-stained face. She jolted upward, grasping her mother's arm.

"We can't find Cecilia," Martina said. Lavenya blinked in disbelief. "She must have thought to go after Lawrence and Antony early this morning, but—"

"Oh, no!" Lavenya wouldn't let her mother finish. She grabbed her coat and donned her shoes, running outside into the harsh winter wind.

"Cecilia!" Lavenya called her name loudly, shivering in her coat. She hurried down the side of the riverbank, calling her name again, "Cecilia!"

She ran alongside the river as the wind blew against her skin, causing her nose to freeze. Her worry turned to panic as she darted into the woods, searching for any sign of Cecilia.

She stumbled on something hard as she tried to climb up the riverbank, landing into the snow. Groaning from the pain, she turned to see what had caused her fall.

A light blue gown was buried in the snow.

"Oh, Lord, no!" She fell down beside the garment, digging through the snow. She felt tears slip down her cheeks as she unearthed her beautiful friend's frozen body.

She pulled Cecilia's stiff, lifeless form into her arms and wept.

# CHAPTER FIVE

## *Fear of the Flames*

"No, Cecilia. Please, God," Lavenya begged God for Cecilia's life. She took her into her arms, pressing her face to Cecilia's long, damp hair. *Why did this happen?* she thought. *Lawrence will be so hurt when he returns. What will we do without her?*

She heard someone walking in the woods and turned, expecting to see her mother. She gasped in surprise. "Lawrence!"

He stopped, planting his boots firmly in the snow. He stared at them with his mouth agape, in disbelief. He stared at his wife.

"She's . . . dead?" He was at their side in an instant, pulling Cecilia from her. He cradled her on his lap and wept. "She's dead!"

Lavenya tried her best to speak, "She went out after you and Antony." She watched her brother weep, rocking back and forth in tears. His crying grew louder as he mourned.

"We couldn't find anyone to help," he said, looking toward her with red, swollen eyes.

Lavenya turned away, hating his distress as he grieved. She placed a comforting arm around him. "Don't blame yourself—she died with the faith," she told him and remembered her mother's consoling words from the previous night. "I suppose it is better to die like this, than at the hand of our persecutors."

Lawrence nodded in agreement, although, it was evident how he felt from his grief-stricken face. "Now we must pray for ourselves." He searched her teary eyes, looking back down at his wife as he cradled her in his arms. "I just don't know how I can live without her."

"Through God's mercy, we'll all rise again," Lavenya comforted him. She turned away from him in tears. "I'll go find Father and the others."

A few weeks later, Lavenya and her mother were cooking, while the boys were running through the room, yelling and shouting.

"What are you boys doing?" Martina asked with a laugh, seeing Fabian, Claudius, and Titus run into the main room, making horse whinny sounds with their mouths. Felicia followed Titus, hanging onto his shirt as they galloped around the room.

"Don't you see?" Fabian asked, racing ahead of Claudius. "It's a chariot race. I have the finest stallions in the front of my chariot."

"I'm riding in Titus' chariot," Felicia told her with a wide smile.

"Playing imaginary games." Martina shook her head. "You children find the most foolish things to occupy your time. Have you even said your prayers this morning?"

The boys and Felicia halted their make-believe chariot race, bumping into each other. "No," they said together and immediately they knelt to pray, clasping their hands.

A smile tugged at the side of Lavenya's mouth as she listened to their sincere prayers.

But their requests of God were far from simple. They asked for God to protect the lives of their families and to end persecution. Afterward, the children jumped to their feet.

"Away to the arena!" Titus shouted with a toothy grin, beginning to race down the darkened tunnel. "I'm going to win this race with my eight white horses!"

Lavenya's smile wavered when she heard his words—she didn't want the boys to ever think that going to the arena was a pleasant thing. It may once have been used for sport, but now it held a much more severe kind of pleasure for the taunting Romans.

Fabian didn't follow the other boys. Instead, he leaned against Martina as she crushed grain in a large, wooden bowl.

She turned to him, patting his cheek. "Why don't you want to finish the race?" Martina asked, playing along with their wild imaginations.

Fabian shrugged and stepped back from her, crossing his arms inquisitively. "Mother, why is it that we keep on praying, but nothing is changing?" Lavenya looked up to study her brother as he continued, "We pray to God, but He doesn't seem to hear us. If He did, we would have food to eat . . . and we don't have any."

"God has kept us alive, dear boy," Martina hastily replied. "And He gives us comfort and peace of eternal life, which is of more importance than this temporal life we have."

"But how can we feel peace when those we love die?" Fabian questioned her.

"We have peace in knowing that one day we'll be united with Jesus and His wonderful Father, to spend eternity with each other in perfect harmony," she said with a smile. "On this earth we cannot live forever, but in the next life, we'll have joy beyond measure. Death is the escape from this life for us—it is not the end."

Fabian nodded, seeming to understand. He then asked, "Do you think Stephen and Cecilia will be there; they were Christians."

She gave him an assured nod. "They were true to God—He will be true to them."

Lawrence bounced Julia on his knee, gently strumming his small, golden harp with the opposite hand. Julia giggled and clung to him to keep from toppling over.

Lavenya smiled at the sight and at the beautiful music that floated through the room. Lawrence's music was one of the only things that seemed to soothe her. Stephen had also taken up the talent and had played just as lovely as Lawrence.

Hearing Lawrence play brought back cherished memories of Stephen. Lavenya stood at the entrance of their dwelling and felt cool wind caress her face. She turned to her mother, giving her a smile. "I'm going to the hill," she said. "Don't fear for me; I won't be long."

Martina nodded. "Go safely. I'll watch Julia."

Her mother didn't try to dissuade her—Lavenya had gone with Stephen hundreds of times before. Lavenya grabbed her cloak, and pulled it securely around her, walking into the night, which was serenaded by the beautiful harp.

She made her way quietly through the woods, going to the hill where she and Stephen had often gone to talk alone, away from the stifling underground rooms. The hill was wonderfully hidden with tall trees and the view of Rome at night was breathtaking.

She let out a sigh as she reached the top, in awe of the flickering lights of the city in the distance. Lavenya let out a wistful sigh as she crawled beneath a large thicket of trees—where she and Stephen had sat many times before, gazing out over the city they had left behind.

She pulled her cloak tighter around her, feeling wind press against her. Tears sprang into her eyes as she viewed the city.

Rome brought memories of the previous year when they fled to the hills, leaving behind everything. Her father had been a Roman nobleman, holding a secure position in sophisticated, Roman affairs. The comfortable life they'd lived had been abandoned when they fled for their lives. They helped some of their friends escape, but were unable to save others.

The emperor, Decius, had ordered an edict that demanded Christians pay homage to the pagan gods of Rome, to show loyalty to the Empire. They had spent fifteen years in peace, worshiping the One God they had come to know—then were forced to flee.

She and Stephen had sat together and talked about their calamity, but also of the hope of God's grace to those who serve Him. Stephen had been such a comfort to her.

*He always kept the faith,* Lavenya reminisced. *He always encouraged me to keep the faith. He taught Julia the way to believe in our Lord Jesus Christ. He will have a great resurrection, just as Paul taught. He fought a good fight, and he kept the faith.*

"A messenger is here—he's got food," Fabian told his father as he came running into the room where they sat in prayer.

"We should have expected someone would come today," Stantius said. "I'll go make sure he is not an enemy in disguise."

Lavenya saw her father stand to greet the visitor, listening in to their conversation.

"Do you know the sign?" Stantius questioned the man.

"Key road," the man said. "I have food for you and your families."

They all listened intently to the conversation above them. Martina placed a thankful hand over Lavenya's, giving it a squeeze. "We needed the food," she said.

Stantius gave him a hearty embrace. "Come, follow me." Stantius led the way to their hidden abode.

Lavenya smiled as Fabian came in, followed by Stantius and a tall, skinny man. His solemn, green eyes lighted as he smiled and nodded to them. He handed the food to Martina.

"God bless you," Stantius thanked him. "Have you any news?"

"Eight more Christians were taken into the arena," the messenger said. "There were men, women, and two children—they were burned. Another man, I suppose who was touched by their sacrifice, was killed and thrown into the flames when he tried to attack a soldier." Everyone around the room mourned with heavy sighs and tears.

Lavenya embraced Julia and cried. *That could have been us,* she thought.

"We must have special prayer tonight for our brothers and sisters. We will have a memorial," Stantius told him soberly. "So, there isn't an alteration in the emperor's edict."

"It still stands," the messenger said, lowering his voice, "There are more patrols in these parts of the terrain. I believe they are more aware of our presence here. I advise caution to you and your families."

Lavenya felt fear enter her heart. She cradled her daughter closer to her.

"Thank you." Stantius took the messenger's hand, and squeezed it. "God bless you and protect you. Send our love and comfort to the others."

The messenger nodded and slipped away.

"He brought fruit from inside the city gates," Martina said, taking out the savory food. She placed an orange to her nose and breathed in deeply.

"You're remembering the orange trees from our garden, aren't you?" Fabian asked, walking up beside her.

Martina turned to him, setting the orange aside. "We'll have plenty of oranges in heaven," she assured him, ignoring his question.

"I hope God will bless the dear Christians who sacrifice themselves to bring us food and news," Lawrence said, coming beside his mother. "Few Christians are brave enough to go into the city."

"And yet, there are braver people—those who were sacrificed today," Antony said, pouring water from the pitcher to drink.

Stanitus nodded, sitting down beside Apuleius and his wife.

"May God have mercy on their souls." He closed his eyes in prayer. "May their testimony be an example for us Christians. May their deaths be a witness to those who killed them. Let them witness God's salvation. It is for all who will believe."

"Amen," they all said together.

"Mama, what did Jesus look like?" Julia asked. Her face contorted in wonder.

Lavenya smiled as she sat beside her daughter, peeling fruit. She exchanged looks with Felicia who sat across from them. Felicia giggled and continued to play.

"Julia, I never saw Jesus," Lavenya said. "He lived a long time ago. All I know is that He was great and He overcame so much with strength from God. He showed us the way to God, so we can live forever with Him in heaven."

"Where is heaven?" Felicia asked, playing with her yarn doll.

"I don't know." Lavenya frowned in meditation, continuing to cut the fruit. "I guess it is wherever Jesus is with His Father. I suppose the angels are there."

"I wanna be an angel!" Julia giggled, causing Felicia to laugh.

Lavenya smiled. "All I know is that heaven is somewhere very glorious. It is a place where God promises us that we will live with Him for all eternity, if we truly are willing to be obedient to Him," Lavenya explained, handing a piece of apple to each of them.

Felicia bit down with a loud "crunch". She smiled. "I'd like to go there someday," she said. "It must be wonderful to just live on and on . . . and never have to see people die."

Lavenya nodded gravely, thinking of Stephen. She took Felicia's hand and smiled warmly at her. "You can be there, but you must serve God with all your heart."

"Yes, that is what Mother tells me." Felicia nodded solemnly as her pretty, blond curls bounced. She smiled with missing teeth. Then she frowned. "But I don't want to die."

"Death is the door that leads us to heaven; everyone dies. We'll all leave his world sooner or later. The Holy Ghost that Jesus gave us is to strengthen us, especially in these times we face," Lavenya explained kindly. She felt as if her heart would break from the saddened look on the child's face.

Felicia let out a sigh. "Will I be burned, Lavenya?" Her lip trembled. "Fire is very hot."

As she started to cry, Lavenya pulled her into a strong embrace, patting her pretty hair. She felt as if she wanted to cry with her, but didn't, knowing Julia was staring at her.

"We must be strong, just as Jesus was strong for us," Lavenya whispered to her. Felicia trembled in her arms. "He will be with us forever."

# CHAPTER SIX

*Stranger at the River*

Lavenya gently tucked her long, brown hair inside her neat braid and lifted a green, glass bottle to pour perfume onto her neck.

"You must give up those oils and perfumes—we are no longer Romans."

Lavenya turned to her father with a sigh as Stantius drank from the water pitcher. "I know, Father, but I adore them. I also miss our heated baths. We live so filthily here."

"Clean hearts is what we should desire," he told her. Lavenya set down the small, glass toiletries, and enjoyed their fragrance with secretive pleasure.

"I suppose I'm not quite as clean hearted as I should be." She turned to her father. "God will have to work on me until I am."

Stantius smiled at his daughter. "As we must, but don't grow weary—going with God is the best journey."

"Where are the others?" Lavenya asked, looking around the room. Martina sat with the women and the girls, but the men and boys weren't in the room.

"Lawrence took the others to help a small group of Christians—they live just down the river. They're building their home underground, but meanwhile, they're gathering in a small bungalow to live and worship."

"Is it safe for them to be exposed?"

"They'll find God's protection. When they've completed their underground dwelling, they'll disassemble the little shack and use the wood for burning."

"Is it impossible to bring them all here?" Lavenya asked.

"The more scattered we are, the less chance it is that the Romans will find us. If they find us all together, we'll all be killed, but if we are scattered, we have a better chance to survive a little longer," Stantius told his daughter.

Lavenya gulped down her dread. *He doesn't sound as if he expects us to live.* She looked to her daughter who was lying peacefully on their bedroll. Her small, dark lashes were turned down on her fair cheeks.

*Sleep on, my child*, she thought. *I pray that you will feel this peaceful all the days of your life. I pray you will never be harmed by Rome's butchers.*

"Will you please wash these in the river? The others and I must prepare the meal before the men return." Martina handed Lavenya a pile of dirty garments.

"If you'll watch Julia for me," Lavenya said kindly.

"Sure." Martina nodded, but caught her daughter's arm. "Wait." She hurried to her and her husband's bedroll to retrieve a long dagger. "I fear for your protection—Romans are everywhere. Take this," Martina ordered, handing the knife to her.

Lavenya studied it and shook her head. "I cannot kill. It is forbidden to commit a—"

"Take it for your protection," Martina interrupted her.

"I have God for my protection, Mother. What can a dagger do for me if I have the power of God covering me?"

Lavenya's words caused her mother to flush. "Bless you for your faith, my daughter." Martina smiled, taking the dagger gently from her. "Then go."

Lavenya hurried out the passageway with the garments in her arms. She ducked out from the entrance, seeing sunlight fading across the sky. The cool spring air greeted her, lightly caressing her face. She smiled thankfully, that the winter winds were vanishing.

Deciding she would move down the river to wash, she scurried along the rocks, careful not to lose her footing. Setting down the clothes on the rocky riverbank, she grabbed the first garment and dipped it down into the chilly water, moving it along the rocky bottom. She watched the dirt from the garment float down the river.

*Just as the dirt is being washed away from this garment,* Lavenya thought with a smile, *so may the sin from the hearts of all emperors be washed clean. Let them turn to us with open arms. Julia would have a better life then.*

Lavenya washed several garments and laid them out to dry on the rocky riverside. Feeling sweat trickle down her forehead, she hastily pushed away her loose hair. She turned with alarm, hearing a horse approaching. She dropped the gown she was washing.

A shadowed figure appeared on horseback, riding out of the thicket on the opposite side of the river. She was unable to move.

"Pardon me, miss." The voice was deep and gentle.

She couldn't see his face in the shadows, only the silhouette of his broad shoulders. She stumbled back up the riverbank.

"Do not be afraid. I mean you no harm," the man told her, riding forward.

"You can't harm me," Lavenya said the words before she could prevent herself. "I have the power of God with me."

The man smiled. "I come in the name of our Lord Jesus."

"Do you know the sign?" she asked with trembling hands.

"Key road."

Lavenya seemed to let out her breath as the man began to ride toward her. As he trotted from the thicket, she saw his handsome face. He had soft, green eyes and black hair. His smile was tender and kind.

"What's your name?" he asked, gripping the reins of his horse.

Lavenya hesitated and thought, *Father would not allow me to openly tell who I am to a strange man. Father must meet him first. Besides, I am a widow now.*

"Never mind," the man said kindly and pushed his horse forward, heading down the riverbank, as if he intended to cross. Lavenya's eyes widened as the man's horse began to slip on the loose rocks. He grabbed the reins as his horse whinnied. The horse tumbled forward, causing the man to fall from the horse's saddle.

Lavenya screamed.

He fell into the rushing river, landing against the jagged

rocks. His head went under the water and bobbed back up again. The man was groaning in pain.

"Oh, God!" Lavenya jumped to her feet and hurried to the edge of the river, panicking. "Are you all right?" she called to him and turned, seeing his horse jump out of the river and take off in a thundering gallop up the cliff. The man watched his fleeing horse.

"Try to swim, or you'll drown!" Lavenya called to him with fear.

"My leg! I think it's broke," the man called back to her as his head dipped back into the rushing water.

Lavenya closed her eyes as she jumped into the water, pushing her arms and legs with all her strength. She swam against the frigid current, praying her strength wouldn't fail her.

The man turned to her fearfully as he sank beneath the water.

Lavenya dove down after him, gripping his arm. With the ease of the river to help her, she lifted him above the surface, pulling him with all her might to the other side of the river, where the clothes were laid out to dry. The man groaned.

Lavenya let out a relieved breath as she felt her feet hit against the rocks of the embankment. She pulled herself out of the river and turned to pull him up behind her as he pushed with all his might. Seeing one leg drag behind him, she then saw it was broken.

"Try to be patient while I get help," she said.

"I'll try." The man gritted his teeth in pain. He gasped for air, spitting up water from his lungs.

Julian felt pain shoot through his leg as he watched the young woman hurry away from him. Dusk had settled throughout the forest.

He gripped his leg, feeling pain shoot up his muscle from the bone protruding out of his flesh. Tears slipped down his face, under the unbearable pain. He closed his eyes, remembering the woman he'd just encountered. He sucked in his breath and spat. Water dripped from the sides of his mouth.

*How brave she was to save me from the river,* he thought. *The current could have taken us both down the river to our deaths. She's quite strong.* He chuckled despite his pain. *And she's quite a beauty. She's unlike the pagan women in Rome.*

He felt himself drifting from consciousness, recollecting his beautiful rescuer.

Lavenya hurried into the room, grabbing a blanket and water pitcher. "Father, you must come quickly."

Stantius took his daughter's arm. "What's wrong?"

Lavenya spoke in a panicking rush, "While I was washing at the stream, a Christian man rode through the woods on horseback. He was flipped from his horse's saddle as the horse tumbled down the ravine. I dragged him from the river. He's badly hurt."

Martina placed a worried hand to her mouth.

"Take me to him," Stantius said, grabbing an old shirt. "We can use this to bandage him."

Stantius followed his daughter downstream until they came to the man. They knelt beside him. Stantius examined his wounds.

"He's lost a lot of blood." Lavenya watched her father shake his head with distress. "Yes, I can see from his clothes that he is one of us." He pulled at a cross necklace on his neck. "We must see that he is cared for."

Lavenya poured water on the man's wounds as her father began to shred the old shirt he'd brought. They began to bandage up his wounds, using the faint moonlight to give them light. Lavenya wiped a gash in his forehead as her father wrapped the man's leg securely.

She looked up, hearing voices in the woods. "That's Lawrence and the others," she whispered to her father.

"Good." Stantius studied the man with compassion. "They can carry him to our home."

# CHAPTER SEVEN

## *Too Pretty to Burn*

The boys crowded around as the men lay the wounded man onto a blanket. "Look at his muscles!" they said together.

Lavenya hid a smile as she nuzzled her face in Julia's curls.

"Yes, he's quite strong." Stantius knelt down beside the man. "He'll have to be strong to come through this injury."

Lavenya set water on the fire to boil and walked to the wounded man's side.

He awoke several times in the night, muttering painful groans. She awoke every time he let out a line of agonizing cries and pulled Julia close to her, patting her curls. Thankfully, Julia slept soundly throughout the night.

The man turned his head slightly and she could see crusted tears on his face, mixed with dirt and droplets of blood. Her heart filled with compassion. She was thankful she had saved him from what might have been a terrible death. He murmured a groan.

*God, please heal this stranger,* she prayed and turned away from him as her mother and the ladies came into the room with the girls.

"How is he doing, Lavenya?" Martina asked. They placed the food they had gathered from the woods beside the fire.

Lavenya hurried to take a basket from her mother. "He's

moaning again."

"I couldn't sleep last night because of that poor man's terrible groans." Lydia wiped a hand through her graying hair with a weary yawn.

"Apuleius woke several times too," Alluvia told them. "I just comforted him until he went back to sleep. We must try to be patient."

"I got scared when he cried out in the night," Felicia said. "I thought he was dying."

"Let us pray he won't die." Martina brushed a hand through Felicia's curls.

"Don't talk about death," Lavenya whispered to them, pulling Julia in her arms.

"It is a part of life, Lavenya," Martina whispered back to her. "Julia must not grow up naive."

"The less she knows about the cruelty of life, the better," Lavenya persisted and headed to the entryway. Martina turned toward her daughter with a questioning frown.

"I'm going to the hill," Lavenya said, walking outside.

"Lavenya is very protective of her daughter. If we are ever captured, Julia will not be safe in the hands of the Romans," Alluvia said dolefully.

"She lost Stephen," Martina explained. "She doesn't want to lose someone else she loves, but she must learn that her daughter's life does not belong to her—she belongs to God."

"Look, Julia." Lavenya pointed to the city of Rome. The sun was shining brightly over the spacious city. "That is Rome—where we came from."

"I don' 'member," Julia said with large, curious eyes.

"You, your father, and I lived in a large house. We must stay here now if we are to serve God," Lavenya explained to her.

"Pretty!" Julia giggled, throwing out her thin arms. Lavenya laughed and embraced her.

"You think the city is pretty?" Lavenya smiled. "You know what?" Lavenya bounced her daughter on her knee. "One day we'll be able to return to our city. God will turn the hearts of our enemies."

"Yay!" Julia giggled again, leaning against her mother's shoulder.

They sat together in the cool shade as the warm spring sunlight surrounded them. Lavenya smiled, thinking of the glorious day when they would return home.

Hearing distant horses, she turned abruptly. Pulling back several tree branches to peer through, Lavenya's heart turned cold within her as she saw Roman soldiers on horseback in the distance. They led a cage-like wagon that was crowded with prisoners.

"Oh, Lord." Lavenya closed her eyes, knowing the prisoners were Christians. She felt tears slip down her cheeks as she gripped her daughter.

"What's wrong, Mama?" Julia asked.

Lavenya quickly let the branches fall back in place. She held her daughter in her arms and hurriedly got to her feet. "Nothing, dear," she whispered to her.

She walked swiftly down the hill.

Julian groaned as he awoke, seeing women standing above him. One of them placed a damp cloth to his forehead.

He immediately felt as if knives had been driven into his leg and throughout his entire body. A moan escaped his lips.

"He's waking, Lydia," one woman said. "Please get me the pitcher."

He felt cool liquid press against his mouth, and it soothed his dry throat. He opened his eyes, seeing a little girl lean over him. She was smiling.

"The handsome fellow is awake," she told them, causing the women to laugh.

"Are you well? I'm sorry, but the other men are away," a woman said. "We're going to try to help you. God will heal you."

Julian murmured a groan. He heard sniffles and turned his head slightly.

A young woman hurried into the room, carrying a small child. It took him a minute to see that it was the same woman who had rescued him. *She's crying,* he thought, hearing her sniffle.

"What is it, Lavenya?" The women surrounded her.

*So, that is her name.* Julian repeated her name in his mind, *Lavenya.*

"I saw a caravan from the hill," Lavenya said.

"Your father!" The woman gripped Lavenya's arm fearfully. "I want you to go see about him and the others. It could have been them!"

Before she could respond, Lavenya ran from the cave in tears. Julian watched Lavenya's mother embrace the women beside her as they wept.

"God will help us," one of them said. "Let us pray they were not taken."

*I will pray they were captured and slaughtered,* Julian thought with little compassion.

Lavenya ran through the woods, crawling over sticks and limbs in her path. She tripped, feeling thorns cling to her dress and tear into her flesh. She groaned, yanking at her dress. Hurrying to her feet, she wiped away her tears.

*God, please keep my father and brothers safe,* she prayed earnestly.

"Father! Lawrence! Fabian!" she called with short breaths.

She felt her heart soar when she heard Lawrence calling back to her, "Lavenya?"

She hurried from the thicket and into a meadow. Seeing that her two brothers, her father, and the other men were still working, she nearly collapsed with relief and exhaustion.

"Oh, God!" She heard her father hurrying toward her. "What's upset you, dear? Are your mother and the others well? What happened?" Stantius quickly helped her stand.

"Father!" Lavenya embraced him with tears in her eyes. "I saw a caravan of soldiers. I thought they'd taken you all."

Stantius released her as she tried to catch her breath. "They captured Christians?" he asked her gravely. When she nodded, Stantius squeezed his eyes tightly shut. He breathed a heartfelt prayer. He turned to Lawrence, Antony, Apuleius, and the boys. Then he turned to the other Christians. They quietly began to lay down their tools.

"We will not work tomorrow," he told them. "We will fast and pray."

"Lord Jesus, please comfort our captured friends," Lavenya prayed softly. "Let them feel Your presence. Give them strength to keep their faith and preserve the salvation of their souls."

Opening her teary eyes, she watched everyone in the room, bowing their heads in prayer. They all wept and embraced. *How long must we weep for the sins of our forefathers*, she prayed inwardly as she clasped her hands. *How long must we endure these pains? How long will it be until You give us the strength to continue our endurance of this suffering, if we must? Save us, Lord. Please, save us.*

Hearing the wounded man moan, she turned. His eyes fluttered open as he awoke. Lawrence hurried to his side, giving him a comforting pat on his shoulder. "Are you feeling well, my brother?"

The man coughed. "Not any better, but you look troubled. What's ailing you?"

"Soldiers captured more of our brothers and sisters, bringing them to Rome," Stantius replied, walking to the man's side. "This could not only mean the death of our captured friends, but that more soldiers will search these areas and take our wives and children captive."

Lavenya watched the young man's face. He closed his eyes painfully, sinking back down onto his pillow. Seeming to let out a sigh, he turned to them with eyes of distress.

"We must pray for the return of our brothers and sisters. God will be victorious over the butchering Roman soldiers," the man said. He turned over to relieve his pain. "God will triumph."

"I've come to believe that as well." Stantius nodded. "Meanwhile, we will try to help you recover from your injury. My name is Stantius and this is Lawrence, my oldest son. What is your name? Where are you from?"

"I'm Joannes," he said. Lavenya watched as the man spoke. "I've come from Rome and I'm traveling among the Christians. I'm searching for my mother. She's taken refuge among our brothers and sisters."

"Let us pray that she has not been taken captive. What's her name?" Stantius asked.

"Celina."

"With this terrible injury, you'll not be traveling anywhere," Lawrence said.

"Yes, I know." The man chuckled and groaned. "But God will heal me."

Lavenya pulled Julia onto her lap and turned as the man spoke. He leaned his head against his pillow. Though his body looked wretched and tired, she saw courage in his eyes. He was just the man they needed—one of courage.

"You're a man of faith." Stantius patted Joannes' shoulder. "Yes, we have much to pray about." Stantius sighed. "As for our captured brothers and sisters, we must also pray for a messenger to come and tell us what has happened to them."

Joannes looked to him. "When was the last time a messenger came to you?"

"Not long ago, a messenger came with food from the city. He told us eight more prisoners were burned. One man that tried to attack a soldier was thrown into the fire," Lawrence said.

"I remember that report." The man's face clouded over with pain. "I was headed back to Rome, not away from it. That's when I had this terrible accident. I was looking for something to eat." He smiled. "I am fortunate that this young woman saved me."

Lavenya watched the man's gaze turn toward her. She met his thankful eyes with a smile, brushing a hand through Julia's hair.

"Who is that pretty, little girl?" the man asked.

"That's Julia, my granddaughter," Stantius stated with pride. "And this is Lavenya, my daughter. Her husband, Stephen Galagus, was killed by the Romans. God rest his soul."

Julian stared at Lavenya. *My scrawny, little brother was married to that beautiful woman?* He let that thought settle in his mind. *Stephen, you always were a lucky scoundrel.*

*It's a good thing I changed my name to 'Joannes',* Julian thought. *Otherwise, they would immediately know who I am. No doubt Stephen has told Lavenya all about 'his wicked brother'. They would know right away that I am not a Christian.*

*I must do just as I was instructed. I'll be well soon. Just as these devil worshippers have deceived my brother and led him to his terrible death, so they all must die by the hands of Rome.* He looked at Lavenya. *Well, not all. She's much too pretty to burn.*

# CHAPTER EIGHT

## *A Stubborn Widow*

Lavenya listened to Julia sing from the adjoining room and smiled. She continued rolling out dough and began kneading it beneath her fingers. Lavenya turned with a start, hearing Joannes chuckle from where he had been sleeping.

"That girl is the happiest I've ever heard." He grinned. "Sorry for startling you."

"It's all right. I didn't know you were awake." Lavenya walked to him with a pitcher of water. "Would you like something to drink?"

"I'm fine." Joannes coughed and leaned back with a groan. "I hope these bones will heal soon. Your father wrapped me up well." He looked down at his bandages.

"Are you feeling well?" she asked, handing him another quilt.

"I'm well—with you by my side."

"I'm a simple widow." Her words were nervous mumbles.

He grinned. "You're a modest widow and one blessed by the Lord. You may call me Joannes."

She was thankful to see her mother enter the room.

"I guess you were awakened by our lovely singer?" Martina asked.

"She has quite a talent, yes." He chuckled—his voice was gentle and soft.

Lavenya turned toward him with a confident smile. "That

talent is from her father. He was a wonderful singer. When he and Lawrence would play for us, we listened for hours."

"Julia loved her father?" Joannes asked her.

Lavenya smiled, lost in her affectionate memories.

"She loved him dearly," Martina said as she placed the bread Lavenya had been kneading into their small, stone oven.

Lavenya smiled. "And he loved her," she told him and examined his leg wound, grabbing more cloth to rewrap his injury. She knew he was watching her.

"Did your husband have family?" Joannes asked. "Were they informed of his death?"

"He had family, but I don't know if they were informed about Stephen." Lavenya turned toward him with saddened eyes as she spoke, "Stephen often mentioned his family. He loved them dearly. He often prayed, even to the last of his breaths, that they might know Christ."

"And they never did?" Joannes asked her.

Lavenya shook her head. "Not that I know of. He said his mother, Theodora, and his older brother, Julian, served the Roman gods faithfully. He never spoke much of his father, only that he died." She turned toward him, sensing his silence. She went on, "He spoke much of his brother. He always liked to tell me of their hunting trips they had as boys.

"Julian loved him dearly, that is, until Stephen found his faith in Jesus."

Joannes turned to her. His voice suddenly sounded very grave. "How tragic for two brothers to separate."

*He seems to be such a caring and compassionate man.* Lavenya smiled. Turning toward him, she was certain that she saw a tear dripping down his face.

"I thought you'd be up here."

Lavenya turned as Lawrence ducked beneath the willow tree. She smiled, turning back to look out over the city. "I feel like I can see the whole world from up here."

"Rome isn't the whole world," Lawrence told her.

"I know it," she replied, seeing that he held his harp. "You've come to play for me? You're just like King David, but you've yet to be a poet."

He chuckled, strumming his fingers along the strings.

"Actually, there's something else I would like to tell you." The tone of Lawrence's voice caused Lavenya to look at him. He was studying his harp, strumming it gently.

"What? It's poetry, I hope," she said.

"No, but it's something like poetry." His eyes danced. "Lavenya, I don't really know how to tell you this . . . I'm going to be married."

"Married to who?" Lavenya studied his rosy face with a frown.

He grinned as he spoke, "There is a young woman who lives among the Christians we are helping. She reminds me so much of Cecilia. Her name is Aria." He hesitated. "Are you pleased?"

Lavenya turned her gaze back to the city, but she no longer smiled at what she saw. "Cecilia has just died, Lawrence. You're already marrying again?" she spoke firmly, feeling tears well up in her eyes.

The strumming stopped. "But I love her; she's a dear woman," Lawrence insisted. "Father has given me his blessing. He says that I may live with them. I can be of great help to their family and the other Christians. They need help terribly."

Lavenya ignored his gaze. "I thought you loved Cecilia."

"I did love her, but I cannot bring her back." Lawrence let out a long sigh. "Aria is a great comfort to me. I thought you'd be pleased."

Lavenya turned to him. "Pleased?" Her voice was filled with emotion. "Cecilia was a dear friend to me."

Lawrence let out a sigh. "She's gone from me, Lavenya."

Lavenya remained silent for a long time. She turned to him with tearful eyes. "I guess you are like David." She folded her arms and shivered.

Lawrence's voice faltered as he stood. "I hope you won't miss me too much."

"I will miss you," Lavenya told him, squeezing her eyes tightly shut. "I just loved Cecilia so much."

Lawrence nodded, holding his harp close to his chest. "I loved her too, but she's gone from me, never to be my wife again. If I could bring her back, I would . . . but I can't."

"So you'll just replace her with another wife?"

"She can't be replaced," he insisted. Kneeling in front of his sister, he placed his arm around her. "She's can't be replaced, just as you cannot be replaced as my sister."

She turned to him and let out a long breath. "I will love Aria as a sister."

Lawrence seemed to sigh with relief. He gave her a hearty embrace. "Thank you. I promise you'll love her."

"I've brought you something to eat, Joannes."

Julian turned, seeing Lavenya leaning over him with a plate of food. He grinned and strained to sit up. He eyed the others eating around the fire as they conversed. He thanked her as she handed the food to him and noticed her red, puffy eyes.

"What's wrong?"

She hastily wiped away another tear. "It's nothing."

"You're crying. Tell me," he whispered, taking a bite of his stew.

"My brother is getting remarried," she whispered, so she wouldn't be overheard by Lawrence who sat beside the cooking fire, talking with the boys.

"You should be pleased."

She gave a weak smile. "His wife just died. She was my dear friend."

Julian studied her pale face. "And it's too sudden for you?"

"Yes, even though I seem to be the only one who feels that way. Both my parents approve. Anyway, I shouldn't be speaking about such things to you." She shook her head and handed him some bread. As she turned, he reached out and caught her wrist.

"Don't let bitterness consume you," Julian told her. "Love is a gift from our Lord. He sent His Son to give us that love," Julian said beguilingly.

Lavenya's eyes faltered under his, and she quickly turned away. She walked swiftly back to where her daughter and Felicia were playing.

He inwardly grinned and he continued to eat. *She doesn't want to allow herself to love again. But I can sense something in her eyes . . . as I can sense it in my heart.*

"There's a messenger outside," the boys reported as they came running in together.

"I'll go see what he has." Stantius stood up from his seat.

Julian watched Lavenya walk outside after her father with Julia in her arms. He waited until they returned, carrying a large basket of fruit and herbs.

Martina hurried to take the basket from him. "Thank God for that blessed messenger."

"He brought news of those Christians Lavenya saw," Stantius told them gravely. "They have not all been killed, but they are all being tortured in the Roman prisons. One of them tried to escape, and was beheaded by Emperor Decius."

The women let out frightened gasps.

Julian saw Lavenya's pained face. He turned away, hating the look he saw in her eyes. *You don't understand how rebels must die at any price,* he thought. *You're fortunate that I've been delayed in reporting your family to the Romans.*

Julian looked away as Stantius continued to talk.

*Do not look so downcast, Lavenya,* he tried to speak to her through his thoughts. *You will not die. The centurion promised to pay me handsomely. Having you for my wife will be my reward.*

He inwardly chuckled. *I dare say you'll hate me, but I'll prove the truth to you in time. Christianity must be stifled from the earth. You'll understand when you see everyone else suffering and you're free. You'll appreciate me for saving you.*

"God bless you." Lavenya kissed Aria's cheek and turned to embrace her brother.

Lawrence gave her a hearty embrace and turned to his wife, taking her hand in his. "God has blessed me more than I have ever dreamed," he told his wife, leaning to kiss her forehead.

Lavenya smiled weakly, seeing that Joannes was staring at her.

"The Lord will surely be gracious to you," Stantius told his son, giving him a proud pat on his shoulder. Martina leaned to embrace her daughter-in-law.

Lawrence walked to Joannes' side and leaned to give him a firm handshake. "I pray you'll have a rapid recovery." Joannes thanked him and wished him well with his new wife.

"Will you come often to play for us on your harp, Lawrence?" Fabian asked, placing an arm around his brother.

Lawrence chuckled, ruffling Fabian's hair. "I'll come often and play for you."

Julia tugged on his cloak. When he turned to look down at her, she reached for him to pick her up. He drew her into his arms and nuzzled her nose with his. "You stay as sweet as you've always been and Uncle Lawrence will return to see you," he promised.

Julia kissed his cheek and threw her small arms around his neck. "Bye, Uncle Lawrence!" Her sweet voice caused everyone to laugh.

"You'd better say good-bye to your aunt too," Lawrence reminded her, setting her down.

Julia raced to her and placed her arms around her legs. She smiled up at her sweetly. "Bye, Aunt Cecilia!"

Everyone fell quiet with dismay.


"Must you cut my hair?" Fabian complained with a pout, sitting in front of his sister.

"Yes. Hold still," Lavenya said, cutting another curl. "You'll look like Samson if you keep growing it."

Fabian chuckled boyishly. "Will I be strong? If I could be strong, then I'd like to have long hair."

"You are *not* Samson." Lavenya smiled.

"Samson obviously wasn't very strong—he fell for a deceiving woman." They turned to Joannes as he spoke, tugging on his hair. "I like my hair."

"You're next," Lavenya told him with a smile.

"I guess I am starting to look unruly."

"At least you're strong," Fabian said with envy.

"You're as strong as Samson, even with short hair."

"If I was as strong as Samson, I could walk," he muttered.

"You'll gain strength," Lavenya assured him.

"Then you can go find your mother."

"You want me to leave?" Joannes asked her. He sat up quickly.

Lavenya smiled. "I didn't mean that," she said.

"You didn't because you like him!" Fabian said, laughing.

Lavenya's eyes widened with embarrassment, causing her hand to lose grip on the knife. She yelped as the blade cut into her thumb.

Julian jumped up, forgetting his injury. He immediately collapsed onto the floor.

Fabian and Lavenya turned away from the cut on her thumb and hurried to Joannes. Lavenya wrapped her shawl around her cut as she and Fabian hurried to help Joannes. He sat up with a grunt.

"Never mind about me; let me see your wound." He took Lavenya's hand.

"It's nothing."

He examined the cut carefully. "It looks like something to me." He looked up at her kindly. "It's deep." He turned to Fabian. "Get some water and a cloth."

Joannes took a knife from his pocket and cut the cloth Fabian handed him. He washed the blood away from her thumb and bandaged the wound securely.

He raised grinning eyes toward her. "Now, you ought to be careful from now on and not let your mind wander."

Fabian snickered, covering his mouth with a bony hand.

Lavenya felt heat rise up the back of her neck. She hurriedly walked from the entrance of their hidden abode and headed to the hill. It was her and Stephen's hill—it always would be.

*Joannes seems to be a good man,* she thought. *But not even death can end the love I feel for Stephen.*

# CHAPTER NINE

## *The Cost of His Mission*

Fabian and the boys ran into the room, carrying two sturdy sticks. They hurried to Julian, where he was lying on his bedroll. He sat up with a groan as they bumped into him, jarring his sore limbs. "We're gonna help you walk, Joannes," Fabian said with a grin.

"Did you chop these from the woods?" Julian examined the sticks, taking them from him.

"I used the ax to chop them," Titus said proudly, pointing a finger to his chest.

Julian studied the two long sticks and turned to grin at Lavenya and the women who were sitting across from him, sewing.

"What do you think, Lavenya?" Julian asked her. "Do you think they'll hold me up?"

"Can you hold yourself up, is the question." She laughed.

"Well, the only way to fly is to try." Julian grinned at the boys and slowly sat up—his leg was wrapped in yards of fabric. He slowly stood to his feet with a grunt and looked down to see the boys' smiling faces. Julian managed to stand on one leg and then groaned, slowly sitting down again.

"Joannes, the Lord has been gracious—you'll be walking soon," Martina said.

Julian grinned inwardly. *And won't I be glad!*

"Then you ladies won't have to hear me grumbling about being bedridden," he told them with a chuckle. "When I can function, I'm not quite so unbearable."

"You're as red as a bright apple in the sunlight, Lavenya," Martina whispered to her daughter as they watched Joannes play with the children, sitting on his blanket.

Lavenya frowned and opened her mouth to defend herself.

Martina laughed. "Don't try to deny it—I see you're taken with Joannes."

"I am not," Lavenya argued.

"He's a good man."

"Stephen was a good man."

"But Stephen is gone from us," Martina pointed knowingly at her. "You cannot deny that he's handsome. And he's strong and gentle."

Lavenya ignored her mother and turned to watch Joannes. He took Julia in his arms and tossed her into the air. Julia squealed, landing back in his arms.

Martina gently touched her daughter's arm. "Stephen wouldn't want Julia to be without a father's love. He would want a strong man like Joannes for you."

Lavenya listened to her mother in silence.

"We must pray that you'll get well, so you can find your mother."

Lavenya listened to her father and Joannes, as they sat together beside the cooking fire. Stantius had managed to help Joannes struggle out of his blankets, so they sat up and talked together as everyone slept. Joannes ate his food in meditation and nodded as the firelight flickered across his handsome face. "I feel God touching me."

Lavenya held sleeping Julia closer in her arms, listening to her daughter's soft breathing as it rose and fell.

"Is your mother elderly?" her father asked.

"She's a beautiful, elderly woman," he said. "My father called her a 'lovely legend'."

"What happened to your father?"

"He died several years ago. I took up his trade—a rug merchant. It gave us quite a large fortune," Joannes told him.

Stantius nodded. "I left quite a fortune when I took refuge here for my faith." Joannes turned toward him. Stantius studied the

56

fire. "I was a silversmith."

"A silversmith?" Joannes asked.

Stantius nodded and folded his hands. "I gave it up to have my faith. I believe Jesus saves me far better than any wealth in this world. My wealth meant nothing to me after the edict was passed. I gave everything away."

"The conversion you felt must have been quite powerful."

"Yes. When I felt the message of Jesus, our wonderful Savior, touch my heart, I realized there is nothing greater than sacrificing everything for the belief I have in Jesus. My family agreed to come with immediate decision. I thank God for my daughter's husband—Stephen was the greatest man I've ever met," Stantius told him.

Lavenya closed her eyes when she saw Joannes turn toward her, looking where she slept in the darkness. Opening her eyes to slits, she saw him falter as he turned away. The pain in his eyes gave her immediate curiosity.

*He has compassion*, she thought. She then frowned as she studied him. *He reminds me of Stephen. He even looks like him.*

"I think he married quite a wonderful lady as well." Lavenya's eyes opened wide when she heard Joannes' words. Her father chuckled beneath his breath as he patted Joannes on his shoulder. "I sense your heart told you that?"

"It doesn't take a heart like mine to realize something as obvious as that."

"Just a wise mind and two eyes." Stantius chuckled along with him. "You're a worthy man. It's been a blessing to have you."

"So you don't oppose of my affection?"

Lavenya waited to hear her father's words.

"Marriage during this time wouldn't be wise—children must not enter a world like this."

"I could be of great help to you and your family," Joannes vowed. "I can work and I have good arms. And I have strength . . . when I'm not broken up."

Stantius chuckled again. "Yes, that's quite evident." Then her father said, "Yes, I approve quite readily."

Lavenya found herself smiling in the darkness before she could prevent herself. *Stephen would not be happy with me,* she thought guiltily. *But somehow, I can't hide what I feel inside. Mother is right—Stephen would not want Julia to be without a father's love. I pray this is God's will.*

Julian sat in the cleft of a large crevice, studying the sunlight that cascaded through the tree branches. He'd managed to limp up the hillside, breathing in the crisp morning air.

Gazing down by the river, he saw Lavenya washing clothes. He grinned as he listened to the sweet hymn she sang.

"May I help you, Lavenya?" Felicia asked as she fell on her knees beside Lavenya.

He watched as Lavenya smiled at the pretty, girlish face beside her, dipping clothes into the rushing water. She handed her several pieces of clothing and continued to wring out the garment she washed. Their voices drifted up toward him.

"You used to have maids to do this, didn't you?" Felicia asked her.

"When we lived in Rome, we had many servants."

"We didn't," Felicia told her and giggled.

"I remember teaching you how to wash when we first came to these hills," Lavenya said and smiled at the memory.

"We lived in the slums," Felicia went on. "I like it out here much better. It's a lot quieter and you can get more sleep in the night. The Roman patrols aren't such a ruckus, either.

"Do you like it better out here?"

Lavenya hesitated and answered with discretion, "My memories of Rome are filled with memories of Stephen—of course, I miss it."

Julian felt a surge of jealousy within him. *Stephen,* he thought, spitting with anger. *You have taken the heart of the most beautiful lady in Rome. That god you believed in must have given you a streak of luck.*

"I suppose I love the countryside because we can worship the Lord here." Lavenya smiled down at the little girl. "I'd rather be in the harshest place in the world and feel the Lord, than live in the finest palace without Him."

*Why?* Julian found it hard to understand. *How can she love a god that causes so much heartache? How can she love a god that allows its own people to suffer; a god that may not even exist? She's putting her faith and trust in something unknown to our gods.*

"Why do we worship God?" Felicia went on to ask, "Why won't He save us?"

Julian waited for Lavenya's response.

"There is no greater joy than to die the same death that Jesus died. God is testing us to see who is willing to love Him and keep His commandments, even by giving up our own lives. We serve God because He is worthy to be praised. We are promised a wonderful reward in Heaven."

*'A wonderful reward in Heaven',* Julian repeated in his mind. *Does that mean she believes in eternal life with her god?* He placed a thoughtful finger to his chin. *The gods of Rome have no rewards. Where will I be after I am dead? Where are Stephen and Mother now? And Valerian? Where will I be after I am dead?* His raging thoughts unnerved him.

Lavenya heard Julia squeal as Joannes chased her and the boys around the room. She watched him take several strides and playfully tackle Fabian.

"His strength is back," Martina whispered to her daughter. They had been sitting with the other women around the cooking fire to make their evening meal.

Lavenya mustered a fluttery laugh and leaned toward her mother. "I'm glad he can play and capture the attention of Julia and the others."

"I see they aren't the only captured ones." Martina gave her a sly smile.

Lavenya disguised her giggle with an unnatural cough, causing Joannes to turn toward her. He released Fabian's arm from his back—the boy fell to the floor.

"Are you all right?" he asked her, standing to his feet. As soon as he was upright, the boys and Julia grabbed onto his legs.

Lavenya and the others laughed. "I was wondering the same about you," Lavenya said.

Joannes grinned. Winking at her, he looked down at the boys and shaped his hands into claws, letting a deep, frightening growl from his throat. The boys began running around the room. Julia squealed and ran toward her, too exhausted to play further.

Joannes looked to Lavenya for her approval.

She gave a hearty laugh, but then her laughter died away when she saw her father walk into the room with Antony and Rufus. He wiped at the perspiration onhis forehead and walked toward his wife, placing an arm around her and kissing her soft cheek.

She placed a hand to his red face. "You're wearing yourself out, Stantius," she said in a scolding tone.

"I'm all right." He searched her eyes with a grin. "I'm not old . . . yet." Stantius turned in the direction of Joannes and the children when he heard one of the boys let out a groan, trying to tackle Joannes again. He chuckled, seeing them for the first time. "Why don't you just give up, Joannes?"

"Never!" Joannes said with a grin, pulling one of the boys from his back.

"Do we have enough food to last until another messenger arrives?" Stantius asked Lydia and Alluvia.

Lydia looked into their pot and at the other things the ladies were preparing. "We have some, but I don't know if we have enough."

At hearing this news, the boys released Joannes, and he straightened his tousled shirt. Fabian walked toward them with a frown, placing hands on his hips. "You mean we might not have enough to eat? Are we going to starve like we did in the winter?"

"No, my son." Stantius hushed him, placing a hand on his shoulder. He turned to his wife. "I won't let us go through that again," he said resolvedly. "We'll pray."

"I know I've been a burden to your family because of my illness." Joannes took a step toward them. "I want to repay you for what you've done for me—you saved my life. I will go to the city and get whatever you need," he said.

"But you must not take the risk," Stantius protested. "It could mean certain death for a Christian to be captured within the city gates."

"God will protect me," Joannes replied with determination. "I have faith in Him."

"I thank God you came to us." Stantius placed a firm hand on his shoulder, and gave it a manly squeeze. "If you do as you say, then you'd best leave before dawn."

Lavenya watched Joannes nod in agreement. Her heart seemed to burst within her with admiration for Joannes—the man she had saved.


"Why do you take such risks for us?"

Julian turned from where he was silently loading his bag to hear Lavenya's gentle whisper. She sat down beside him. *Because I want to marry you*, he thought, but he answered differently, "I must sacrifice myself for my friends who have sacrificed for me."

"Here—this is all we have left." She handed Joannes a small bundle. He took it hesitantly. "It's wheat bread," she whispered.

He shook his head, placing it back into her hands. "You'll need whatever food remains to keep you going until I return."

"You'll need strength for the journey," she insisted, trying to hand it to him.

*Stubborn lady you are*, Julian thought. *I'll have plenty of bread in the city.*

"If you will not eat it, Julia will," Julian told her. He stood to his feet. Julian watched the others as they slept soundly. "Dawn will be breaking soon."

"This is something I wrote." She handed him a piece of paper. "It isn't finished."

"I'll read it while I'm away," he promised her.

"Please stay safe." He nodded, studying her pretty face in the darkness.

*If you knew the truth of my errand, you wouldn't be wishing for my safety. But you'll realize the importance of my mission once you and Julia are safe with me in Rome.*

His thoughts must have betrayed him for she asked, "What's wrong?"

"Nothing." He managed a shaky smile. "I'll return to you soon." He placed a nervous hand to her chin and kissed her cheek. He studied her blushing face, feeling his heart soar. "Stay safe and I'll return with food." Before she could reply, he hurried into the darkness.

Julian had wanted to tell her much more, but knew he

couldn't . . . not at the cost of revealing his mission.

# CHAPTER TEN

## *"Why Must We Suffer?"*

Julian found himself dozing beside his campfire, serenaded by his hissing campfire and the hoot of an owl. The wind rustled the hair on his forehead. How he longed for a horse—he would already be in the comforts of Rome.

"What about this thing she wrote?" he asked himself aloud, taking out the note Lavenya had given him. He saw lines of verse were written and he read them aloud, *"Our garments cast shadows on stone. The weight of our chains causes our hearts to groan. We sigh as we long to be free. Our children cry, but cannot whisper a plea."*

He folded the letter, trying to understand the words she'd written, seeing it was obviously the beginning of a poem. He sat there for some time, thinking on her words.

"Will you enjoy this campfire with another?"

At hearing a voice, Julian sat up so quickly that he felt his head spin. He stared at an elderly, humpbacked man in front of him, holding the reins of his horse. Julian reached for his knife.

"Just a minute," the man said. "I'm neither a bandit, nor a beggar—just want a place to warm my feet . . . and my food." He hastily dismounted.

Julian slowly lowered his knife. "Who are you?"

"I'm a friend." The man set down his sack and tied the horse's reins to a nearby tree. He sat down across from Julian, pulling off his hat with a warm smile. "My name is Marcus and I'm traveling back to Rome. I've been traveling the country, but I must return to my business. Who are you, young man?"

"Julian Galagus. I'm heading to Rome as well."

Marcus took several bundles of food from his sack. He offered a piece of bread to him.

"Thank you." Julian accepted it with gratefulness.

"So…what brings you to this part of the country?" Marcus asked him, placing his food over the fire to warm it.

Julian sat back, taking a bite of his bread. "I've been commissioned by the Roman centurion to scout these hills for rebels."

"For the Christian rebels?" the man asked and chuckled as Julian nodded. "I am not one of those fools. I believe they should follow our gods, but I don't want to take up a hand against them. You do what you must, but I would suggest you refrain from doing them harm."

"Why is that?" Julian frowned, studying the old man.

"I don't see how killing others can help us," the man replied. "I believe converting those fools back to worship our gods would be a greater mission than just killing off our own nation, but what do I know?" The man chuckled. "Perhaps you're right."

"I know I'm right." Julian stared into the fire. "Those 'fools', as you call them, will only infect our country. They are the influence that resulted in the death of my mother and brother."

"So your heart is in what you're doing, huh?"

"Yes," Julian said.

The man nodded. "You must follow your heart, yes."

Julian thought of Lavenya. "But I've found a woman I love from among them."

"Love!" The man took a long sip from his water skins before he replied, "How can you love a woman from the people you despise?"

"She's beautiful."

"Aw, yes." The man chortled with sarcasm. "That explains everything."

Julian turned toward him. "She is my dead brother's wife. I've vowed to save her from her death. I'm going to appeal to the centurion to give her to me as my wife."

"She is your reward?"

"Yes." Julian hesitated. "I know she'll take it hard losing her family.

"Why these Christians insist on causing more pain for themselves is difficult for me to understand. This belief is strange, indeed."

Marcus nodded. "As I have come to learn myself. They search and they search and they search for the answers their heart is longing for, and that is something I can't blame them for. I don't believe that Jesus was the Son of God, but what I do know is that those people are quite courageous. I've witnessed their persecution myself."

Julian nodded solemnly, remembering Valerian. "As have I." He then sighed. "I must leave early in the morning to be there before dawn. I lost the centurion's scroll in a river when I nearly drowned—I expect I'll face trouble for that."

"Well, all you can do is hope for the best, Friend," Marcus encouraged him.

"I need to get to Rome." Julian let out a long sigh.

"I need to get some sleep," the man replied and chuckled, eating the last of his meal. "Many thanks for allowing me to rest here awhile."

"Think nothing of it," Julian answered him.

The old man laid down to rest.

He sat for a long while and watched the stars in the sky, unable to rest. Julian looked toward the man's horse and then down at Marcus as he snored softly. *I need to get to Rome,* he thought. *This old man doesn't need that horse as much as I do. I have a mission to accomplish anyhow.* He pulled a bag of money from his pocket, and placed it beside Marcus. *That'll be my payment, so I wouldn't be accused as a thief.*

He quietly gathered his things, and placed them in his sack. He untied Marcus' horse and took the reins in his hands. Mounting the horse, he looked down at Marcus. He felt sudden compassion for the man, but quickly disposed of it.

*Many thanks for your horse, "Friend",* he thought heartlessly and started away in the darkness. He couldn't believe his luck.

Julian slowed his pace as he neared the fortified camp that

was situated at the edge of the city. He studied the lighted campfires as the soldiers dozed at their posts. He slipped from his horse. He searched the horizon.

"They won't let me in without the centurion's scroll," he told himself. He looked to a single campfire that was away from the others, where a soldier was polishing his sword.

He tied up his horse and ran across the field in the darkness, approaching the back of the soldier. Running forward, he pinned back the soldier's thin arms, placing a hand to his mouth. He grabbed the man's fallen sword and placed it at the man's throat.

Julian realized the soldier was a few years younger than himself. The soldier looked terrified as he stared with large eyes up at him.

"Have no fear. I'm not here to take your life . . . if you don't alert the guards." Julian hesitated. "I'm on a special mission for your centurion. I need to get into the camp and speak to him, but since I lost the issue, they won't allow me to enter the camp. If you'll help me, you'll be rewarded handsomely. Do you agree to that?"

The soldier nodded with a gulp.

"Good." Julian released him. He looked to the tent behind them. "Can you change fast?"

The soldier nodded.

"Hurry. I need to borrow your armor."

The soldier went into the tent and came back, carrying his armor for Julian. "If they catch you, they'll kill us both," the soldier told him.

"They won't," Julian insisted and placed the man's armor about him. He turned back to the soldier. "I'll bring these back to you before you miss them." Julian then hurried back to his horse and mounted. He rode to the entrance of the camp and the soldiers waved him inside. Julian mustered a sigh of relief as he started for the centurion's tent.

He suddenly heard shouting behind him. Turning, he saw soldiers riding after him with torches. He knew the soldier had betrayed him. He spurred his horse into a full gallop, riding swiftly through the camp.

Upon reaching the centurion's tent, he dismounted and tried to hurry past the guards. Several soldiers grabbed him. He fought to release himself. He saw the soldiers ride up toward him and halt.

"What is the meaning of this?" he heard someone shout.

Julian turned, seeing Caspian slip from his horse. Julian tried to jerk himself free from the soldiers. "Caspian, it's me, Julian Galagus."

Caspian took several steps toward him as he fought from the soldier's grasp. He chuckled and raised his hand to the soldiers. "Let him go."

Julian jerked free from the soldiers grasp and approached him.

"So you've had a long journey, I suppose?" Caspian asked with a chuckle.

"It's been quite arduous." Julian nodded. "It was so costly that I lost the scroll, which entitled my commission."

Caspian shook his head with a chuckle. "You risked your life to return?"

Julian nodded, wiping sweat from his forehead.

Caspian chuckled. "You can rest in my tent. At dawn, I'll take you to the centurion."


"I look pretty, Mama!" Julia studied her reflection in the ripples of the river.

Lavenya watched the lilies slip from her daughter's hair and float into the rushing water. Julia laughed and sank back on her knees to watch the lilies float downstream.

"You're the most beautiful girl in this countryside." Lavenya pulled her daughter onto her lap, causing several more flowers to fall from her hair. She kissed Julia's flushed cheek and sighed, watching the water below them.

Julia turned to look at her mother. "Can we go to the hill? Wanna see Joannes!" she gushed.

"It's late, and we have to return home. You'll see him soon. He'll return with food in a few days." Lavenya pushed several loose curls from Julia's forehead. Julia leaned against her with a pouting nod and lodged her thumb into her mouth.

"I miss him too." Stantius sat down beside his daughter, crossing his long legs.

"G-andpa!" Julia said with glee and reached for him.

Stantius chuckled and took Julia onto his lap, wrapping his thin arms around her.

Lavenya studied her father's weathered face. "I miss him too," she said.

"You miss him enough to be his wife?" Stantius met her gaze. Lavenya frowned at him, pointing toward Julia. She mouthed a rebuke to him.

"She is too young to understand," Stantius whispered to her. Lavenya ignored him, turning her eyes to the sunset sparkling across the river.

"He's loyal and strong," Stantius continued. "He'd be a good man for you."

Lavenya still kept her face turned away from him. Stantius leaned forward.

"He's not bad looking, either."

She turned toward him without hesitation. "I know."

"You know?" He studied her. "If he asks you to be his wife, you will?"

"I've thought about it."

"Have you?"

"Yes." Lavenya turned back toward the setting sun. "I just watched my brother marry hastily after Cecilia's death . . . I don't want to do the same."

"It's been many months since Stephen's death."

"I know, Father."

"The more men we have to assist us, the better," Stantius replied and leaned closer. "I feel we may be leaving soon. I've talked it over with the men and your mother. The Romans are scouting this area far too much. I believe we'll head to the north for less hostile country."

"What of Lawrence, Aria, and her family?" Lavenya asked.

"They are skeptical. The farther away from the city we go, means the farther we move away from food and supplies that we need. It takes a lot of faith to make such a journey."

"Others have done it," Lavenya reminded him.

"Many have died," he agreed and added, "But many also have saved themselves."

"God will provide for us—He always has."

"Sometimes God does things that are beyond our understanding." His deep, blue eyes looked solemn. "Death may be a good provision, even though it doesn't seem as such."

"Sometimes I ask God, 'Why must we suffer? Haven't we suffered enough?' And it's then that He always seems to reply to me, 'When I was on the cross to die for you, did I ask My Father, 'Why must I suffer?' No, He didn't."

"It's at those times I know I must go on, no matter the price I have to pay."

Stantius placed a hand to his daughter's shoulder. "Those who will suffer with Him, will also reign with Him."

Lavenya nodded, seeing Julia had fallen asleep in her grandfather's arms. He held her small face to his chest and turned toward the river, watching the flowing water.

*I pray that if Joannes is to be my husband,* Lavenya thought with a rush of anticipation, *I pray that he will be as dedicated and wonderful as my father.* She placed an arm around her father's thin shoulders and leaned her head against him.

It was just as they had done many times when she was a child, when they sat together on the roof of their Roman villa.

# CHAPTER ELEVEN

*According to the Riches*

Caspian gave a deep, throaty chuckle. "She's a beauty, you say? Are all those meager, Christian women fair to the eye?"

Julian turned to face him. "Are you thinking of converting?"

"If it is as you say, then . . . yes."

Caspian and Julian shared a wry chuckle. They sat together in the marketplace, surrounded by Roman citizens. They were seated around a large table, eating quality lamb. Julian sighed contentedly, enjoying being back in his social comfort.

"The centurion was pleased with your work?" Caspian asked him.

"Yes." Julian took a large bite of his food. "He has agreed to give Lavenya as my wife. He's also agreed that I may bring Julia here, for the child can't discern the truth for herself.

"He told me to bring them the food I promised them and to stay until I find all the locations of those who they associate with in the hills."

"How long do you think that will take?"

"Not long." Julian grinned. "They stay in touch, despite how scattered they are."

"They're like a ramped plague in the hills." Caspian chuckled again. "I knew you were the man we needed when I found you. It's a terrible pity you were wounded with a broken leg and had to stick it out with the rebels. Yes, a pity, indeed."

"A pity? I was waited on like a king," Julian said with a long swig of his drink.

"So they're gracious to strangers?"

"Yes," Julian said. "I suppose they'll love anyone, especially those they can pollute to believe as they do."

"I'm glad to see you're still loyal to our emperor."

"Does that surprise you?"

"Not at all." Caspian gave him a wide smile. "I know a loyal man when I see one—I guess that's why the centurion has me scouting for soldiers."

Julian sighed, leaning back in his chair. "I'm eager to return and claim my bride and child."

Caspian fell silent before he replied, "Doesn't your conscience smite you to have Lavenya's love, but have your own hidden intent?"

Julian slugged him with a chuckle. "Why are you being such a softy? You're a soldier!"

Caspian didn't laugh. "I've seen many things in my life, enough to harden me." He paused. "But loving someone is quite different. There's a bond in love that is sacred—even a crude soldier knows that. I had a wife once, you know."

"What happened to her?"

"She died at the birth of our child. The child died too. I regret many things now that my wife has passed. I regret everything—a kinder word I could have spoken, a loving deed I could have done. There are many regrets I store inside.

"I've been hoping for another chance to come along, so I could make it up to a second lady, but nothing has happened. I pray to the gods, but I haven't gotten an answer."

Julian took a long swig of his drink. *I tolerated this man when he was in a better mood. I have enough guilt on my conscience—I don't want to sit with a scum bucket of woe.*

He leaned forward. "Cheer up, my friend. It can't be as bad as you make it." He placed a hand on Caspian's shoulder. "And what would you suggest I do? Tell her what I intend to do to her family and have her hate me?"

Caspian hesitated. "I'm sure there's a lady here in the city worth catching."

"But none of them equal this lady." Julian nudged his arm. "Now, shake yourself from this pity and eat your lamb with herbs. It looks delicious."

"You don't have to tell me twice." Caspian chuckled and took a large bite before he said, "Not telling you how to run your life, but I suggest you find another lady, if you want to have a peaceful home. A mad wife is worse than a thousand wild horses." They chuckled together.

Julian merely shook his head. "Silence, Caspian. I have no time to put up with lectures," Julian chided him. "By the way, I must make one more errand before I go back into the wilderness. I want to finish my food in peace."

Caspian looked curious. "What might that 'errand' be?"

"To purchase a ring for my bride, you fool!"

Lawrence purchased several goods from the Roman marketplace, and placed them into his sack. He went over in his mind all that his father-in-law had asked him to get from the city.

*I hope no one can hear my pounding heart,* Lawrence fretted. *I almost regret that I agreed to this, but I must do it for Aria and her family. I must make the sacrifice.*

*God,* he prayed, *please get me back to my family without being detected.*

"What may I do for you today, sir?" a peddler asked him.

"I'd like to purchase your spices and bread, if I may."

"Here you go." The man handed him the food politely.

Lawrence thanked him with several silver coins. He turned, surveying the busy marketplace. He studied people who were eating across the busy street. He spotted a soldier sitting with a lavishly dressed man. A wave of panic filled his chest.

*Joannes? Surely, it can't be him!*

He waited and watched the conversing men, ducking behind a fruit stand. He studied the wealthy man's face—his features were distinctive.

He slipped into the crowded street with unwavering certainty.

"It's good of you to come visit us while Lawrence is away in the city." Martina embraced her daughter-in-law and kissed her warm cheek.

"I've wanted to visit you for some time." Aria embraced Lavenya and leaned to give Julia a kiss.

Julia wrapped her thin arms around Aria's neck. "I love you, Aunt Aria." Lavenya smiled, thankful that her daughter had taken heed to her reproof concerning her aunt's name.

"You're leaving?" Martina asked.

"Yes, Father said he would meet me at the river, so I wouldn't have to walk home alone," Aria said. "He should be there waiting on me."

After they bid Aria good-bye, she slipped away under the cover of darkness. Lavenya listened to Aria's soft footsteps hitting the ground above their heads.

"Lawrence has given us a wonderful daughter-in-law," Martina praised, bending to stoke the fire. "I pray Stantius returns with wood soon. I'm worried about him being out alone in the woods ever since . . ." Lavenya felt her heart constrict as her mother's voice faded.

"I know," Lavenya said. "I'm anxious every time Fabian goes running through the woods with the boys, but I know it's hard for them to stay in this crowded place."

"That is quite true. I'm glad when we can get some peace and quiet," Lydia agreed, coming to warm some water on the fire. She held several scrolls in her lap.

"What have you got with you?" Lavenya questioned her.

"Just some copies of Paul's letters." She opened one of them before speaking, "I thought I might read a little to Felicia before going to sleep tonight."

"Could you read to Julia?" Lavenya asked hopefully.

"Of course!" Lydia bent to take Julia in her arms. She walked with the two girls to their blankets, where she sat down to read to them.

Lavenya sat beside her mother as they listened to Lydia's sweet voice, reading the letters as if she were reading a prayer.

Martina sighed. "She's reading my favorite letter—the letter to the church of the Ephesus."

Lydia continued to read, ". . . *To the praise of the glory of his grace, wherein he hath made us accepted in the beloved:*

*"In whom we have redemption through his blood, the forgiveness of sins, according to the riches of His grace;*

*"Wherein he hath abounded toward us in all wisdom and prudence;*

*"Having made known unto us the mystery of his will, according to his good pleasure which he had purposed in himself."*
She paused before continuing to read.

Lavenya smiled, thinking over the line she loved, ". . . *According to the riches of his grace."* She studied the fire in meditation. *We are not rich with the things of this world, but with the things that we are to gain from the next, just as Paul promised us. It may cost a very high price, but in the end, it will be worth everything, even our life. 'The riches of his grace'.*

Her thoughts were interrupted when Fabian ran into the room, shouting with joy, " Joannes is back . . .and he's got a horse loaded with stuff!"

"You faced no opposition?" Stantius asked him while they all ate dinner.

Lavenya turned to Joannes. He took a sip of his drink before replying, "It was simple after I got through the city gates. I've learned that peddlers often find it easier to barter. And they don't ask questions, only of the contents in your purse."

Stantius chuckled. "I'm glad for your sake and ours that you were unharmed."

Lavenya felt her face burn as she saw her father give her a sideways glance.

"Where'd you get the horse?" Fabian asked.

"I was wondering that myself." Stantius turned a curious face toward him.

"I found a compassionate man," Joannes explained. "Unfortunately, his wagon had sunk in a riverbank. He had two fine horses, but of one he had no use. I asked to pay for it, though, I hardly had the means. The man merely offered it to me."

"God blessed your journey," Stantius said. "I thank you for what you've done for us, Joannes. I don't know what we would do without you, with Stephen and Lawrence gone."

Lavenya felt as if her heart would beat out of her chest. She smiled at her mother and turned to look at Joannes. She frowned, seeing a strange look in his eyes as he stared into the fire.

Julian looked up to see Lavenya studying him.

He looked away and thought, *I hope she doesn't realize what a coward I am. Her poor father is pouring his heart out in thanks to me and I will soon take his life, and that of his family. And I just told him a bald-face lie. Still,* he thought, *this is what I must do—for the sake of Rome.* His heart seemed to ask, *What about your sake? What about Lavenya and Julia?*

He wished his conscience would leave him alone. Still, in the silence of his mind, of which he dared not reveal, his heart smote his seared conscience.

# CHAPTER TWELVE

## *The Traitor*

"Your father told me you might be up here."

In the darkness, Lavenya heard Joannes' voice from within the trees. He walked through the thicket. "You frightened me. I thought you were a soldier." Lavenya fell silent as he sat down beside her, gazing at the city.

"It's a wonderful view of the world from up here."

Lavenya turned toward him. *"Rome isn't the whole world."* Then she paused, feeling her heart beat rapidly within her. "Father sent you up here to find me?"

"Yes." He gently took her hand. "Julia is asleep. I was wondering what keeps you awake at this hour of the night."

Lavenya turned her gaze to the city. "I come here often to think." She felt the wind flutter through her hair. "I feel the presence of God in these hills, now more strongly than ever."

"You speak to God here?" he questioned her.

"No. I come to hear Him speak to me."

A long silence passed.

"And does He?"

"Sometimes."

They sat in silence for a while. Lavenya felt as if her heart would burst. She remembered the many nights she and Stephan had shared the peace she now felt.

"What has He told you?" Joannes asked her.

"He gives me comfort and strength to go on. He tells me that He loves me and that I must not be afraid of what may happen to

Julia or me. I know He has a purpose for us."

"Indeed, He does—for all of His people," Joannes replied quietly.

"Just before you came, Lydia was reading to the girls before bed."

"Oh?"

"She was reading a reprint of Paul's letter that he wrote to the Ephesians. She read a line that says, '. . . *we have redemption through his blood, the forgiveness of sins, according to the riches of his grace'*. I thought about it long afterwards." She turned to him, squeezing his hand. "He has given us so many riches, Joannes."

He searched her face. "Yes, He has."

"You know, we left everything in the city. We gave up what we had for the Lord. We gave up our riches, but now we have something greater . . . ." Lavenya felt her eyes watering. "We have forgiveness of sins and the riches of God's grace." Lavenya felt tears rolling down her cheeks. She felt his arms encircle her.

Julian's heart stirred within him as she cried. He caressed her hair as she wept. Pushing away the thoughts that invaded him, he pulled back from her.

"God has blessed us with great riches," Julian told her, hoping to comfort her any way he could. "He has given us forgiveness and grace."

"I'm sorry," she hastily apologized, wiping her eyes.

"Don't apologize." He took off his cloak, and handed it to her to wipe her tears.

Julian chuckled and thought inwardly, *This woman is so modest, sweet, and even more beautiful when she cries.*

"Lavenya," Julian said with a long sigh, "I believe God has given us great riches . . . to me personally, and if I could ask anymore from Him, I would ask for your love."

She turned hastily to him, pulling the cloak away from her face. He smiled, searching her beautiful face.

"And you've asked my father?" she questioned him.

"He's given me his blessing. I came here to seek yours. He said as soon as we agree upon it, he'll join our hands in marriage."

Julian pulled a small ring from his pocket. Taking her hand, he watched the delight in her eyes as he slipped the ring onto her finger. "Will you be my wife, Lavenya Galagus?"

She was so surprised that she couldn't speak, but he knew from the sparkle in her eyes that she was giving him the answer he longed for.

The very next afternoon they were married. The room erupted in applause as they sealed their marriage vows with a loving kiss.

After the small ceremony, Julia ran up to Julian with her arms open to embrace him. "Uncle Joannes!"

Lavenya laughed as she hugged her parents. "No, Julia," she told her daughter with a laugh. "This is your father." Julia frowned with confusion.

"You'd better be good to my sister, you understand?" Fabian chided him, coming to place a brotherly hand on his shoulder.

"You know I will." Julian rubbed a hand through Fabian's hair with a chuckle.

"I wish Lawrence could have been here," Stantius said, embracing his son-in-law.

"He probably anticipated this anyway," Julian said.

Julian embraced Martina, wishing with all his heart to be with his new wife and daughter in his Roman villa. Instead, he pushed his thoughts aside. *I'll let these fools have their joy with "their new son",* he thought. *I'll wait a while . . . then I'll complete my mission. I don't want to spoil their happiness too soon.*

He watched his wife's beaming face as she twirled Julia around in her arms joyously. *I will wait. I want to see that beautiful smile on Lavenya's face a little longer.*

"We'll be back." Lavenya heard her husband say as he walked up behind her. "The men and I are just going to see how Lawrence's folks are doing, and if he's returned. Don't miss us."

"How can that be possible?" Lavenya asked, turning to embrace him.

"Pray for strength," Joannes teased, kissing her sweetly.

Lavenya watched him walk outside with the others. She turned, hearing her mother laugh. Martina shook her head at her as she washed her hands in a basin. "I'm glad to you see you're in love with that man."

"I find it impossible to be any other way," Lavenya said dreamily.

"You'll find it will grow easier, or harder as the days go on. This is only the third day, mind you," Lydia said.

Lavenya laughed to ignore her pessimism and hurried to her daughter. "How could it grow worse with a wonderful man like him?" She took Julia in her arms. "Would you like to go with me to wash?" Julia giggled and nodded happily.

"Yeah!" Julia hurried to gather several garments to wash, and handed them to Lavenya as her mother carried the large basket. She started through the lighted passageway and let out a frightened gasp, running right into someone. Julia shrieked.

She felt strong hands catch her by her shoulders as she dropped the basket she carried. Looking up to utter an apology, she saw it was her brother.

"Lawrence!" she exclaimed.

But his face looked grave. He hurried past her without a word, embracing his mother at the entry of the passageway. She and the others had rushed outside, hearing Julia's cry.

Martina let out a relieved sigh and embraced him. "Lawrence, how good it is to see you!"

Releasing her, Lawrence pulled back and searched the room. "Where's Father?" he asked in an abrasive voice.

"He and the men just went to see if you'd returned. Oh, I'm so glad to see you. Did you face any danger? Did you bring any food?" Martina's words came out in rushed sentences as she searched his troubled face.

Lawrence tightened his jaw. "I must see him."

"What's wrong?" Martina's face then lightened. "We have wonderful news, Lawrence. Your sister and Joannes were married! I wanted you to be here, but—"

Lawrence turned toward his sister. "It appears I'm too late."

Lavenya furrowed her eyebrows as her brother approached her, taking her shoulders in his hands. He searched her face, looking more troubled.

"I hesitate to tell you this." He cleared his throat. "But when

I was in Rome, I saw Joannes dressed in Roman attire, talking with a Roman soldier as they ate in the marketplace."

Lavenya's frown deepened. "What are you talking about?"

His face looked grave. "Lavenya . . . he's a soldier."

Lavenya pushed his hands away. "He can't be!"

Martina grasped her son's arm. "Surely, it was someone else."

He shook his head definitely. "It was him, Mother. I'm sure of it."

"No, it couldn't have been him, Lawrence!" Lavenya felt weak, doubting every word he spoke.

"It was him, Lavenya. I'm telling you the truth!"

"Was he in disguise to bring food to us?" Martina asked, pulling her granddaughter into her arms as she started to cry. "What are you saying?" Lawrence's jaw tightened with anger. "I'm saying he's a traitor."

Julian sat with the others at the campfire as Stantius spoke with Aria's father and the other men. He quietly sipped his water, wishing he could be back at their underground home with Lavenya—she was rarely far from his thoughts.

*I need to get a better knowledge of the other hideouts of the Christians,* he thought to himself, eating from his stew pot as the men conversed. *Then I can return and bring the soldiers here to have them captured. I can return home with my wife and daughter.*

The thought of returning home pleased him greatly. He relished the thought of working his trade and spending his nights on the veranda of his estate. Now, he imagined spending those nights with his beautiful wife and sweet child.

His thoughts were shattered as he felt a strong arm grab him by his throat. He felt himself being choked as he was yanked backward onto the ground and punched.

He fought his attacker, swinging with his fists. A moment later, he heard Stantius and the other men shouting. He felt the strong man release him.

Wiping blood from his nose, he turned to see Lawrence. Several men had pinned him down.

"What is the meaning of this, son!" Stantius shouted.

Lawrence jumped up quickly and pointed a finger at Julian. "That man has conspired against us! He's a traitor, Father!"

Julian's heart felt as if it had dropped to his feet. *How does he know?*

"Joannes is a fine, young man, and my son-in-law!" Stantius exclaimed. "Explain yourself. You know that violence is against what we believe. Jesus was not a man of violence, though, He was shown violence."

Lawrence dusted off his shirt, never moving his angry glare from him. "That man has shown us violence, indeed!" he shouted.

"Why would you accuse me of such a thing? I've never hurt any of you. You're my family. You saved my life!"

Lawrence took several steps toward him. "I saw you eating with a soldier in the market—you cannot deny it!"

"You're mistaken. I went to Rome to bring food to Lavenya and her family, not to indulge myself with pleasure," Julian defended himself, knowing he must.

They took two steps closer to each other, angrier than before.

Stanitus rushed forward. "Lawrence!" He gripped his son's arm. "Surely you saw someone else in the city. Why must you rush to conclusions so quickly, son?"

Lawrence took a step backward from Julian, turning to his father.

Stantius placed a loving hand on his son-in-law's shoulder as he spoke, "Joannes is one of the most loyal men I know. He has proven his devotion to this family and we will not cast him away due to some accusation that surely is a misjudgment. Romans look alike."

Lawrence shook his head with angered frustration. Without a word, he rushed past his father and hurried into their home, with his wife following him.

Stantius looked apologetically at Julian. "Take no offense to what he's said. He's a headstrong, zealous, young man . . . just as you are."

# CHAPTER THIRTEEN

*Helping an Enemy*

Lavenya wiped tears from her eyes as she saw Joannes and Stantius walk into the room.

"Tell me it isn't true," she pleaded.

Julian took her into his arms. "Lavenya, how could I betray you?"

"Lawrence has mistaken Joannes for a Roman that he saw in the city." Stantius let out a sigh as he embraced his pensive wife. "He attacked Joannes at the camp."

Lavenya listened to her parents talk to each other as she buried her tears in Joannes' shirt, releasing her fears. She crumbled in his strong embrace, whispering her thanks to God for relieving her troubled mind.

"I know Joannes is a good man. I would never doubt him." Stantius released his wife. "I just hope my son will learn to make better judgments."

Lavenya felt Joannes caress her hair and whisper words of love to her.

"I love you too," she replied as he wiped her tears away with a gentle hand.

Julian listened to his wife's fluttering snore. She flinched as she tossed in her fretful sleep. He placed a gentle hand on her arm and she stilled. He let out his breath and stared at the rocky ceiling above them. Turning on his side, he cradled Julia as she slept. Her small face was burning with warmth as she lay curled on her side.

Julian was thankful everyone was asleep after their long night in conversation. Now, he didn't have to worry about who was watching him.

*That was close tonight,* he thought with a relieved sigh. *I must say it's a surprise that Stantius defended me. I must be a better dupe than I thought. Caspian would be proud of me. I'm not certain Mother would if she were here . . . but what does that matter?*

*I have taken the oath of my life and given my sacred word to Rome. That is something that cannot be broken, no matter how much pity I feel for Lavenya's family.*

He clenched his jaw. *The first one they're going to capture is her fool brother!*

He listened to the others sleeping around the room. He saw Fabian lying on his back on a patch of straw not far from them. He imagined seeing Fabian's skinny body nailed to a stake.

He shivered inwardly and cast the thought aside.

"You must forgive my brother," Lavenya told Julian as he took her hand. They walked together through the woodland, hoping to spend some time alone.

"I already have," was his amicable reply. "I can understand how someone would make a misunderstanding of something."

She smiled. "I'm thankful you're not offended. Father was so embarrassed. Lawrence can be an angry brute when he's determined."

Julian climbed over a fallen tree and then gave her his assistance. She thanked him. Julian turned to look up at the sky as he heard a rumble of thunder above them.

"Do you think it will rain?" Lavenya asked him. "Should we head back?"

"We'll be fine," he insisted. He grinned as she bent to pick a flower from the forest floor, and placed it in her hair. "You're so beautiful, Lavenya." She smiled and squeezed his hand as they continued to walk through the woods.

"Are you still going to search for your mother?" she asked him.

"I know God will bring her to me," Julian replied, hoping his face wouldn't betray him. *My real mother is dead,* Julian thought to himself. *I wish I could tell you the truth.*

"I wish I had the faith you have."

Julian wanted to ignore her statement. Inwardly he grumbled, *I have no faith in your god, Lavenya.* He turned sharply as Lavenya stopped in the path.

"What is that?" She pointed toward a small clearing, where a ramshackle building stood.

"Let's go see." He gripped her hand as they walked through the clearing, seeing the building was badly destroyed with singed boards.

"Someone must have set fire to it," Julian said.

"Who would do such a terrible thing?"

"Maybe it was—" Julian's words were cut short as the clouds broke overhead and rain began to fall. "Come," he urged as the rain began to fall harder. "We'll take shelter in this little building until this passes over."

They entered the small structure, seeing bits of debris and a few wooden chairs that lay broken and scattered around the room. Julian approached the front of the building as Lavenya began to pick through the rubbish lying around on the dirt floor.

Julian caught his breath, seeing a small, wooden cross shoved beneath a pile of waste. He slowly picked it up, and rubbed his finger along the edge of it, wiping away the dust.

*So this is their symbol—the cross.* He felt his heart constrict as he held the cross in his grasp. *Don't be deceived to believe their lies,* he rebuked himself. *Be strong.*

His throat tightened as he choked out the words, "This must have been a place of worship."

Lavenya approached him and studied the beautifully carved cross. "Do you think the soldiers destroyed this place?"

Julian handed the cross to her. "Probably."

He bent down, running his hand through jumbled mess on the ground. He pulled a shawl from the mess. Lavenya screamed. They jumped back.

A cascade of bones went rolling onto the ground. Julian threw down the shawl.

Lavenya sat down on a dusty bench and leaned back, closing her eyes. "I can't bear to look at this terrible tragedy. I want to forget that there's a body in here."

"Try to rest. I'll wake you when the rain stops," Julian told her, hoping to have some time alone to think.

Julian walked to the window, watching the rain pour to the ground, gathering in puddles on the forest floor. He stared at the rain until he heard her soft snoring. He walked toward the wooden cross. He clutched it in his hand and walked back to the window, looking out at the rain.

He felt tears running down his cheeks. He didn't understand the strange feeling that stirred his heart.

"Why hasn't Lawrence come around since he's been back?" Fabian asked and sank down beside Lavenya as she continued to stir porridge over the fire.

"He must be embarrassed at his outburst when he returned to the camp."

"I don't see how he could mistake Joannes." He hugged his knees. "Joannes is one of the best fellows I know. He isn't a traitor."

"Why don't you take Julia to our place on the hillside and teach her some of your studies," Lavenya suggested.

Felicia threw down her yarn dolls, running toward them. "May I go?"

"Take her along and let her help you." Martina patted her son's head as the children marched toward the woods.

Lavenya followed them. "And make sure you hide if you see soldiers."

"Yes, Mama," Julia replied with a gurgle as they darted away.

"I hope the other children heard that."

"They'll be fine," Lavenya said knowingly. "They need to be outdoors. Fabian knows how to stay safe—he went hunting with Stephen many times."

"Joannes, what are you doing up here?"

Julian turned from where he'd been gazing at the city, sitting beneath the willow tree, where he and Lavenya had pledged their love. Fabian and the children hurried toward him.

"Your sister told me this is a wonderful place to meditate," he said.

"Are you talking to God here, like she does?" Felicia asked.

Julian shook his head. "I'm listening." *To my heart*, he thought inwardly.

"I know Lavenya hears from God," Fabian said, sitting down beside him with the girls.

Julian ignored his question. He took Julia onto his lap and kissed her forehead. "What are you children doing up here? Spying on me?" Julian asked them.

Fabian took out several scrolls from his carrying bag.

"Lavenya asked me to bring Julia up here to teach her some of my studies. Felicia wanted to come, so I had to bring her along," Fabian said, with little interest in his second companion.

"I've studied some myself in the past." Julian took a scroll from Fabian. "I can help you with the studying," he offered.

Felicia looked up at him curiously. "You studied in Rome?"

"I've studied many places. We were once wealthy people. My father was determined to have an educated son."

*That is partly true; Father was very well educated,* Julian thought to himself. *He trained me with a well- rounded knowledge of all the Roman gods.*

"We don't need this scroll," he told the children with a grin, handing it back to Fabian.

Fabian gave him a questioning frown. "We don't?"

"I can teach you what I learned as a boy up here," Julian said, pointing at his temple with his finger and grinned. "I will teach you all something new."

Julian sat with the children, teaching them the movements of the seasons and the rapid changes in weather and climate.

He captured their interest so well, that even Fabian stopped squirming. He propped his elbows on his knees, cupping his chin in his hands. Felicia and Julia listened also, taking in the warm sunshine.

Fabian suddenly jerked forward. "What was that?" he asked.

"What was . . . what?" Julian asked with alarm.

Fabian leaned forward. "Do you hear that . . . that noise?"

The children and Julian waited pensively as they listened for the sound Fabian heard.

At first, Julian heard only the swaying of the trees in the wind and the birds. Then he heard a hollow groan. He leaned forward, holding Julia tighter in his arms. "It's coming from down the ravine." He frowned. "It sounds as if someone is hurt."

"We must go and see who it is," Fabian said, immediately jumping to his feet.

"Wait for me," Julian commanded him.

They followed him down the steep side of the cliff.

Julian paused, searching all around the forest for a sign of the victim they had heard. He stiffened, seeing a man faced down below them, sitting beside a tree. He was gripping his leg.

"That's Lawrence!" Fabian said.

Julian hesitated. *That man already hates me and wants me dead. If I go near him, he'll try to harm me, but if I refuse to help him—these children will relay my neglect to Lavenya and the others. I must help him.*

"Let's go see about his wounds," Julian said with a choked voice.

They crawled down the cliff until they reached the forest floor and all hurried to Lawrence. He groaned and squeezed his eyes tightly shut.

"What happened to you?" Julian asked.

At hearing his voice, Lawrence jerked away from him. But the pain he felt kept him from saying anything. He merely groaned and tried not to cry.

"Get . . . away from . . . me," he finally spewed, hissing a line of angry retorts.

The muscles in Julian's neck tightened. "I'm here to help, Lawrence. Don't get angry at me. Tell me what happened," Julian demanded.

Lawrence ignored him and sat up, leaning his back against the tree. He gripped at his right leg.

"It's broken," he finally said and muttered a groan. "I tripped and fell from the cliff."

"Okay, if you'll allow me, I'll bring you back to your home," Julian offered, taking off his cloak. "I know how you feel. I've had my leg broken too."

He took a knife from his pocket to shred his cloak. He began to wrap his injured leg, but Lawrence didn't respond. He merely fell limply against the tree and groaned again.

"If you refuse, you can stay here," Julian told him. "But if you'll allow me, I'll help you make it back home, so the others can tend to you there."

"Fine," Lawrence spat through his teeth, hardly able to tolerate the pain.

"Okay, we'll help you stand."

Julian signaled for Fabian to grab one of Lawrence's arms, while he grabbed the other. Together, they helped him stand as Julian carried most of Lawrence's weight on his shoulders. Julian looked down to the girls—they were terrified.

"Felicia, you stay close behind. Carry Julia and Fabian's bag," he ordered. "Fabian, try to give most of the weight to me," he said. "We'll go slowly toward his home." Julian grunted, burdened with the weight of Lawrence.

*The weight of my enemy,* he fumed.


"He'll need plenty of rest," Aria's father told Julian with gratitude.

"Yes, he'll need it." Julian turned to look at Lawrence's weary body as he slept on a small cot, surrounded by the children and his wife. Aria gave him a drink of water.

"I can't thank you enough," the man told him warmly.

"I was glad to help," Julian said, but he hoped his expression wouldn't betray him.

Julian grumbled inwardly. *I care nothing for him, but still I helped him—although I don't feel a bit of pleasure in it. I do feel a terrible ache in my back.*

"Come on, children. We must return before it gets late," he called to them.

They began to follow him out.

Julian paused, hearing movement from the cot. He looked

back and saw Lawrence struggling to sit up with the assistance of his wife.

His forlorn face looked pale in the dim light. "Sorry I misjudged you, Joannes," Lawrence called weakly. "I'm sorry, my friend."

# CHAPTER FOURTEEN

## *Whispers in the Night*

"As Jesus sat with his disciples and said, '*Take, eat; this is my body*', so we will eat the unleavened bread." Stantius held up the bread and closed his eyes.

Lavenya and the others bowed their heads. Lavenya opened one eye as she prayed, seeing all the children bow their heads, murmuring their silent prayers.

"We bless You, Father, for Your sacrifice of love by which You have redeemed us," her father prayed. Lavenya said the words along with him in her heart. "We come before You to give You thanks and honor. Bless our lives here and help us to flourish under Your mercy and grace, which You bestow upon us. Amen."

Lavenya watched her husband take the bread from her father and tear a piece off for himself. He handed the bread to her, and she took a piece. Handing a piece of the bread to her daughter, she closed her eyes, giving her own blessing of thanks.

Opening her eyes, she placed the warm bread to her lips. She noticed Joannes was studying her intently.

Julian chewed on his bread in meditation, listening to the others quietly praying.

He excused himself and walked to his blankets, lying down. He closed his eyes for several minutes. He jumped, feeling a hand on his arm.

He stared up into Lavenya's beautiful eyes. "Is everything all right?"

"Fine," he said quickly. "I'm just tired."

She smiled warmly at him. "Just checking on you." She patted his hand before joining the others around the fire.

*'Tired' is not the word for it,* he thought to himself. *I'm . . . worn out.* From what, he couldn't have explained. *I'm worn out from trying to be something I'm not,* he rationalized.

Though he was tired, Julian couldn't sleep. He finally sat up, realizing that everyone had finished their meal and gone outside. He was alone in the room. He knelt down, reaching for his bag that was securely hidden beneath his bedroll. Going through his bag, he searched for the scroll of his commission that the centurion had given him.

*I need to be reminded of my duty,* he thought resolutely. *I can't be swayed by these madmen who call themselves Christians.* He furrowed his brow. *I need to reread what the centurion has assigned. I need to clear my thoughts.*

He pulled out the scroll and sat back, reading the words that would lead Lavenya's family and the other rebels to their death. His heart was filled with renewed passion as he hastily rolled up the scroll. Placing it back into his bag, his hand felt something hard and unusual. He gripped the object and pulled it out.

His heart leapt. His mind reeled. His hands trembled.

It was the wooden cross from the abandoned temple. And he had not placed it there.


Julia tried her best to sit still for Lavenya to braid her hair. She giggled, fiddling with a ball of yarn that was interwoven in her finders.

Lavenya kissed her forehead and listened to Joannes and Lawrence. They sat together beside the cooking fire, talking.

"It was good of you to come with us to visit our friends," she heard Lawrence say.

"They're very kind people. I was hoping to find my mother there."

"You'll find her, by God's grace," Lawrence comforted him, placing a kind hand on his shoulder. Lavenya smiled at the sight.

"I'm terribly sorry for ever misjudging you," Lawrence apologized. "I acted out on my instincts, and not my wisdom. That day you helped me—I can never thank you enough."

"I owed it to you. You've been good to me," Joannes replied.

"Not always." Lawrence chuckled. "I wanted to kill you a while ago, but I realized that isn't what Jesus would have done. I want to try to be like my Savior, if I ever expect to live with Him and His Father."

Lavenya continued intertwining her fingers into her daughter's hair. "Yes," she heard Joannes say. "It's a very noble cause."

"I find it very difficult at times," Lawrence admitted with hesitation. "This life is a battle. You either strive to do God's will, or you strive against it. I'd much rather strive for it and have a better outcome." Lawrence chuckled at that. "Yes, strive for it, indeed."

"Are you enjoying life where you are?" Joannes asked. "How are the other Christians?"

"They're very encouraging to be with." Lawrence grinned. "They give me strength to continue on, especially my wife. Aria is a great joy to me. Cecilia was a great joy that was taken from me, but I love Aria as well." Her brother's words pained her.

"How did your wife die?" Joannes asked.

"She fell ill this past winter . . . and she just got weaker. I left to find a physician to come see about her. Though I searched and searched, I never found one. It was hard to deal with her loss. I was certain God would heal her."

"But He didn't?"

Lawrence fell quiet for a while. Then he said, "Sometimes, we expect God to do what *we* want Him to and when He does what *He* wants, we think He's failed us."

"And do you think that?"

"Sometimes I want to," Lawrence admitted. Then he nodded. "But I know that God knows best for my life, and everyone else's. He knew it was her time—it didn't matter how I felt about it. God understands far more than we give Him credit for." Lawrence paused. "Perhaps He saw something coming in our future that He knew she couldn't bear.

"In this day and time, it isn't in choosing to die, but how to die. I would much rather see my wife face a gentle death, than at the mouth of a lion, or the torture of flames."

Lavenya felt her heart tremble as he continued, "I've heard the grisliest stories of what they do to Christians. The soldiers often have the women exposed in the marketplace, or do worse." Lawrence stared into the fire. "I'd much rather see my wife die the way she did."

"And do you fear that Aria will face those terrible deaths?" Joannes asked. His voice seemed to waver as he spoke.

Lawrence let out a long sigh. "God must know she can face whatever comes. God will not leave us to suffer, even in the midst of the persecution. He is full of mercy and grace."

Before going to sleep, Julian thought of all Lawrence had told him. His mind raced with overwhelming thoughts.

*Lawrence is a wiser man than I thought. His ideals are quite . . . courageous.* He immediately tried to push away his thoughts, but they wouldn't leave him. *He's risking not only his life, but that of his wife and maybe his future children. He's sacrificing himself for a god he cannot see. He has no proof that this god even exists. How can they worship a god with uncertainty such as that? How can they? How can Lavenya be so blind?*

Julian reached in the darkness until he found his wife's hand. It was calloused and hardened, unlike those of the Roman women he'd previously known. He squeezed her hand before releasing it. He turned over on his side and listened to her soft breathing.

*Why am I here?* He questioned himself. *I know I must fulfill this mission, but it would be easy to escape.* He then chuckled in his mind. *You fool,* he told himself. *No one ever escapes from the Empire and breathes another breath. I must remain loyal if I want to live.*

He peered through the shadows of the room, seeing the children sleeping on their hay patches. Across from them, Stantius and Martina slept. Stantius held an open scroll in his grasp from where he'd fallen asleep, reading copies of Paul's letters.

*That poor man is deluding himself. He had great riches in Rome. Why would a man give up so much for so little? Why would he worship a god that he doesn't even know?*

Julian placed a hand to his forehead, wishing he could fall asleep.

He closed his eyes, feeling himself slowly drift asleep. His mind was filled with strange dreams. Julian yanked the blanket up to his neck.

*"Julian, Julian . . . you shall know Me."*

Julian shook himself from his restless sleep. He reached for his knife with sweaty palms. He yanked it from the sheath. Looking around the room, he saw that everyone was asleep. He quickly turned to his wife—she lay fast asleep. *Strange*, he thought. *No one here knows my name is Julian.*

He slowly lowered his knife with trembling hands. He searched the room for where The Voice had come from.

He let out a sigh and lay back down against the straw, repeating the words he'd heard, *'Julian, Julian. You shall know Me. You shall know Me. You shall know Me.'*

He couldn't fall back asleep as the words continued to go over and over in his mind. He stood up, being careful not to wake his wife. He grabbed his cloak and hurried out into the woods, taking in the crisp air that blew through the trees. He sat down beside the entrance of their home. He placed his face in his hands. He jumped at the hoot of an owl.

"Who are *You* that I should know?" he asked in desperation.

Then he heard The Voice again, *"You shall know Me . . . for Who I really am."*

# CHAPTER FIFTEEN

## *Unseen Savior*

"Were you suffering from a dream last night? You were so restless, I was worried. Then you stopped—I was too tired to see if you'd fallen asleep," Lavenya said. She sat down beside Joannes and handed him his morning meal.

"Maybe it was the restless day I had," he said.

Lavenya watched his face turn troubled. Thinking he was right, she hurried to wake Julia. "Do you plan to sleep all day long? You must wake up so your Uncle Fabian can teach you."

Her daughter turned over sleepily, with her tangled curls in a mess. "Mama," Julia mumbled, still sleepy.

Lavenya took her daughter in her arms. She sang sweetly to her as she picked up a brush and began to brush her hair. She used a water basin to wash her face and arms.

Noticing Joannes move by the fire, she saw him place the last of his food into his mouth. He walked out the entrance without a word.

"Where's Papa going?" Julia asked her mother as she sang to herself.

"I don't know." Lavenya suddenly felt worried. "He didn't sleep well last night."

*Something is wrong,* Lavenya thought. *He's troubled about something.*

Lavenya walked toward her husband as he brushed his horse. "That man gave you a strong horse."

Joannes turned to her and took her hand. "He won't be strong if I can't supply him with enough grain to eat." Joannes pulled her toward him, placing his arms around her shoulders.

She smiled up at him. "God will provide."

He nodded slowly. "Yes . . . I believe He will. He has already," he said. "But, I'll have to go to the city for grain soon."

Lavenya felt a wave of dismay. "I don't like you going to the city." She gingerly touched his coarse cheek. "It's hard enough for us to stay safe away from the soldiers. In the city, you're among them."

"Have no fear for me. He will provide, remember." He leaned to kiss her. "I love you, Lavenya," he told her tenderly, dropping the reins from his hands.

Lavenya immediately felt the familiar tingling feeling enter her heart. "And I love you." She gripped his hand. "I'm just worried that you'll be taken from me someday because of your fearless travels."

"I fear every time I leave you and Julia. I fear for your life. I promise that no one will ever harm you." He tenderly caressed with her hair.

"And what of the others?" she asked him. "Don't you want their safety?"

He nodded, but said nothing.

"Papa, wait!" Julia called in a childish garble as she followed Julian through the tall grass. He chuckled under his breath, turning to see her running toward him.

Julian looked ahead to see Fabian, bounding down the riverside in his long, ungainly strides. In his hand, he held two long fishing poles, a box of meat bits, and bait. Fabian turned to look back over his shoulder impatiently. "Hurry up! This is a nice place to fish!" He called, plopping down on the riverbank.

Julian waved him on and turned, grabbing Julia into his arms. Giggling, she squirmed until they reached the place where Fabian sat waiting for them.

"The water looks deep enough," Julian said after looking into the river.

"I'm gonna catch enough for everyone to eat!" Fabian stated

proudly.

"Catch a big one and you just might."

Julian helped him set the bait on the end of his pole. Julia sat beside them, finding more interest in digging her fingers through the mud and plucking up the grass.

Fabian tossed his line into the water, letting out an excited, "Whoopee!"

"Quiet, Fabian! You never know when soldiers are near."

"They wouldn't take me." He laughed. "I wouldn't let them take me."

"What makes you think you can stop their swords?" Julian questioned.

"I'll punch them in the stomach and give them a black eye. I'll kick them, crush them into the ground, give them a big wad of spit, and I'll—"

"You'd better not let your mother hear you say that," Julian interrupted with a laugh.

"I've told her that myself." Fabian sat up straight and propped his fishing pole between his legs. He placed his chin in his hand. "How long do we have to wait for the fish to bite?"

"Until they do," was Julian's quick answer. Then he smiled. "But we can talk some."

"What's there to talk about, Joannes?" Fabian looked uninterested. "All I see is a bunch of trees and some water—no fish." He studied the water, jutting out his lower lip.

"There's a lot to see in the outdoors." Julian tweaked Julia's cheek. "You have the grass and the sky. The breeze tickles your face and hair."

"Bugs, too!" Julia giggled, dangling a worm in Julian's face. He chuckled, knocking the worm from her hands. "Mother would scold you, Julia. Anyway, I didn't think little girls liked to touch worms."

"Julia has all us boys to be with—she's different," Fabian explained, tugging at his pole with little patience. He grinned. "Felicia still doesn't like worms though."

"Wo'ms! Wo'ms! Wo'my!" Julia garbled, grabbing handfuls of mud.

Julian sank back on his elbows, turning his gaze toward the rolling clouds. "I've never liked them much, either."

*You couldn't have a view like this in the city,* he thought to himself.

"I'm tired of 'worms'. Let's talk about something else," Fabian complained.

Julian chuckled. "But you offer nothing to speak of."

"There's a fish!" Fabian suddenly shouted, leaning forward to watch a large fish swim near his floating bait.

"Be still and he might take a nibble on your line," Julian instructed.

Fabian sat erect, daring not to breathe. They waited in silence as Fabian's pole bent a little. He gave Julian a large grin. "It's tugging," he whispered and held his breath again.

"Stay still." The line tugged again and they both sat transfixed.

"I wanna see," Julia said.

Julian turned briefly, seeing her scoot closer toward the edge of the riverbank. She took another step forward. He grabbed for her, but he didn't move fast enough.

She tumbled into the rushing waters below with a muted cry.

"Julia!" they screamed.

Fabian dropped his fishing pole, letting it tumble into the stream. They both struggled to the edge of the river, seeing Julia's body being carried downstream.

"She can't swim!" Fabian cried, gripping at Julian's shirt.

Julian jumped into the river.

Fabian ran along the riverbank, making sure he could see her small body in the water. "We're going to get you out safe, Julia!" he screamed to her, crying as he ran.

Julian swam with all his might, remembering the terrible incident he'd experienced when he had nearly drowned. He wouldn't let Julia die. He couldn't.

Amid his raging thoughts, he saw her thrash in the water a few feet ahead of him. He suddenly remembered The Voice he'd heard - *You shall know Me for Who I really am.* The words were clear in his memory. He dove beneath the surface of the water, feeling terror grip his heart.

*If there is a real Savior out there somewhere,* he prayed, *this would be a good time to know Him.*

"Did you hear that?" Lavenya breathed to her mother as they both sat transfixed.

"Yes," Martina said, turning toward the others with terror.

"Julia!" they said together, stumbling over each other through the wooded tunnel.

Lavenya felt panic grip her heart as she tripped through the woods, heading for the stream. "Oh, Lord," she prayed. "Please let Julia be safe!" Tears sprang to her eyes. She gripped her mother by her hand as they ran.

They first saw Fabian, running beside the river, yelling and shouting to Joannes.

"Joannes is in the water!" Martina said, out of breath.

"Oh, Jesus!" Lavenya cried loudly when she saw Joannes swimming in the rushing waters and Julia's small body being tumbled down river. Julia cried out for help, causing Lavenya's heart to break.

They all ran toward Fabian, shouting to Julia and Joannes as their words overlapped each other. Fabian trembled as tears spilled down his cheeks.

Lavenya cast her eyes to Joannes as he swam in the water, turning in all directions to search for Julia.

Her little body disappeared from sight.

"No!" Lavenya uttered a violent scream from somewhere deep inside her as she watched Julia sink beneath the water. She collapsed, feeling her father's strong arms catch her as she fell.

"Pray! Lavenya, pray!" her father's haggard voice called to her.

Lavenya broke free from his grasp and jumped into the water, where Julia had been, hitting her knees against the rocky riverbed. Swimming back to the surface, she gasped for air, feeling water fill her lungs. Coughing, she thrashed her arms violently in the water, trying to grab for her daughter's little body that she was certain was there somewhere.

Her hands gripped a pile of weeds.

She let out a painful scream, feeling Joannes' strong arms

encircle her. Her weak body fell limply against him as she cried, "Julia! Julia!" She buried her face into his soaking shirt.

"It's my fault." Joannes's voice broke, "I let her die."

"No." Lavenya placed her arms around him, hating his pain that intertwined with hers.

Julian scrambled from the rushing water, trying to help his wife get a footing on the slippery bank. His heart pained him as he slipped in the mud, trying to hold onto his wife. She felt weak under his grasp. A knife seemed to be thrust into his heart.

He saw a large flash of light. He turned his eyes to the clouds, but heard no rumble in the sky, no sign of rain.

"What was that?" Martina spoke up—obviously she'd seen it too.

Julian ignored it. He could only bury himself in his grief.

*Our child is dead,* the grisly thought continued to echo into his thoughts. *I let her die. You!* he accused The Voice that had spoken to him with hatred, *I knew You weren't real.*

"Lavenya! Joannes!" Julian turned, hearing Fabian as they struggled to the shore.

His eyes were glowing as he tugged at their sleeves. "Julia! Come and see!"

Julian looked at his wife. Her face was soaked with tears. Mud was smeared down her face and hair. Her lips trembled as she cried.

"Hurry!" Fabian urged them, grabbing Julian's hand. "I must show you something!" They felt uneasy at his urgency as they ran.

They followed him until he entered a small thicket. Julian looked at Fabian—he was beaming. His heart leapt, but he doubtfully cast his hopeful thoughts aside.

He and Lavenya reached him first and looked in the direction he pointed saying, "Look!"

Julian sucked in his breath in disbelief. He looked at his wife.

Julia sat on the grass, looking up at them.

"Julia!" Julian and Lavenya ran to her, grabbing her up in their arms as they hugged and cried. Everyone grouped around them, embracing and crying.

"Thank You, God!" Stantius hugged his daughter and son-in-law with overwhelming joy.

Julian pulled Julia back from his chest and Lavenya wiped her damp hair from her face. The child was more beautiful than ever. The glow in her eyes was unlike any child. She smiled at them.

"We thought you'd drowned. How'd you get out of the river?" Julian asked.

"A man," she told them. "He moved me."

Julian's voice shuddered as he spoke, "W-what man?"

Julia shook her little head, as if in a dream. "He moved me… from the water," she said in her childish voice, and looked directly into his eyes. Julian felt something strike the center of this soul.

"Then He left."

# CHAPTER SIXTEEN

## *A Strange God*

Julian watched the light from the cooking fire send reflective shades of gold across the floor, until it came to rest where Julia slept soundly. Her delicate features were peaceful as she lay beneath the warmth of her blankets. Visions of her eyes, when she'd told him what had happened to her, would not give him rest. It vexed his memory.

He picked up the bread he'd warmed by the fire, and placed it in his mouth. It warmed his senses, but not his heart. The hungering need of his soul still cried out.

*I must get back to Rome,* he thought, *before these people persuade me to push aside my beliefs. I don't want to waste my life as they're doing. What I saw today . . . it was very strange, but anyone knows that could never happen—anyone with common sense.*

"You remember that poem I gave you?" Lavenya sat down beside him. His thoughts immediately faded at the sight of his wife.

"I never forgot it," he told her, placing his arm around her.

"Listen to what I just wrote." She pulled out a scroll from her pocket and began, *"We sacrifice ourselves for the opportunity to live. Our blood, we are willing to freely give. We know it will be worthwhile in the end. If we continue, God's grace He will send."*

"You have a great talent, Lavenya." He gave her arm a squeeze. "He certainly has given us grace today."

"If I did have 'a great talent', I would know what else to write. This poem isn't completed," Lavenya complained, mustering a sigh.

"In time you'll get the rest of it," he promised her, kissing her forehead.

"Maybe you can write the rest—we'll write something together," she told him with a smile. He chuckled under his breath, but didn't reply.

Lavenya cradled her arms around her daughter. Even being half asleep, she thanked God again for saving Julia.

*It was none other than a miracle,* she thought and smiled in the dim morning light. *God did a miracle for us. Thank You, God, for allowing our faith to be renewed in Your wonderful way once more. You are a great God!*

*You show favor to Your children and You help us when we are afraid that we've reached the end. It's then that we realize You were there all along, to hear our cry.*

Turning to Joannes, she sat up quickly—his place beside her was empty and the covers were thrown back. *He must have gone outside,* she thought, but found a note on his pillow.

Sitting up, he unfolded the small note and began to read, *"My love, don't fear for me. I left before dawn for safe travel. I'm on my way to the city for grain and a few supplies that I know Stantius has need of. Do not worry about me. I know God will protect me. Please keep Julia safe until I return. I love you. Joannes."*

Lavenya placed the letter beside her and felt a strange feeling enter her heart—something wasn't right. *He's never left without saying anything.*

She slipped out of her blankets and crept outside. She looked for his horse. It was gone. She sat down beside the river and watched the morning light sparkle across the water. Placing her arms around her knees, she placed her chin on her knee. She sighed uneasily, unable to explain his hasty disappearance.

*He must be hurting over what almost happened yesterday. This may be his way of getting away to be alone,* she consoled herself.

"I got me a saved girl! I got me a saved girl!" Fabian cheered as he crawled around the floor with Julia on his back. The other children followed, cheering and laughing over the joy of their little friend who nearly drowned in the river.

Julia beamed under their attention, being happier than she'd ever been before. She jumped from Fabian's back and joined hands with Felicia, dancing with her around the room.

Martina laughed and handed her needlework to Lavenya to finish. "Listen to those sweet children, singing praises to the Lord. It touches my heart."

"They should want to sing." Lydia sat down beside them. "God saved that little girl in such a miraculous way. No man could have done it, but our Lord in Heaven did."

Lavenya shuddered. "I don't know what I would have done if she would have drowned."

"Poor Joannes was already blaming himself before we found her," Martina said.

"Where is Joannes?" Lydia frowned, just thinking of him.

"He left before dawn to travel to the city." Lavenya continued her mother's sewing. "He wrote me a note—he had to get some grain for his horse. I expect he'll bring back some things for Father too. It's so easy to lack things we need here."

Lydia shook her head in dismay. "It's getting more dangerous to travel in this territory. Fewer messengers are coming to give us the reports."

"We must pray that God will protect him on his journey. He's such a brave man." Martina placed a hand on her daughter's hand, and gave it a tender caress.

"Yes, your Roman estate is lovely." Caspian looked around the large courtyard, taking in the lavish view of Julian's home. He walked near a large fountain, dipping his hand into it. He cast his eyes on the marble sculptures and art adorning every corner of the villa.

Julian sighed. "You can imagine how I've longed to return."

"You'll soon have a beautiful wife to rule this villa, I assume?" Caspian grinned and followed Julian into a spacious parlor.

"Beautiful, indeed." Julian grinned as he began to eat. "But remember, I can rule my own house, Caspian." They laughed heartily.

They took their seats at a large table, where servants had placed gold and silver plates, filled with fruit and meat. Caspian took a sip of wine from his glass.

"Have the soldiers been assigned?" Julian asked him.

"We're leaving to find the Christians tomorrow morning. I have your map of their locations," Caspian said.

"I, for one, am thankful I can finally stay here in the comforts of Rome."

"It must have been hard to live in the wilderness with those rebels." Caspian leaned forward and studied him, taking a bite of an apple in curiosity. "Tell me of your journey."

"It was quite strange, as you could imagine." Julian hesitated, studying his food as if he found it fascinating. "Strange, indeed."

Caspian dipped his bread in honey and savored it in his mouth. "How so?"

"It was unlike anything I've ever seen. I've been hearing... strange voices."

Caspian stopped chewing. "You're not being converted, are you, Julian?"

"Of course not, but you must know what I saw. You'd also agree there were strange happenings among those Christians."

"Go on," Caspian urged as he began to eat again.

Julian waited until his servants left the room before he continued, "Lavenya and I went into the woods and we found a little church that had been destroyed. I found a cross there and strangely, I heard The Voice speak to me. A few days later, I found the same cross in my bag that I left at the little church."

"Didn't you suspect Lavenya of putting it there?"

Julian shook his head. "No, I kept that bag hidden—no one ever saw it. In fact," Julian paused in his thoughts and turned to the door, calling his servant.

One of them returned with his bag. Julian looked to Caspian—he was waiting nearly at the edge of his seat. Julian opened the bag and pulled out the wooden cross.

Caspian's eyes widened. "You're right—that is quite strange."

Julian then handed the bag back to his servant, placing the

cross inside it. He went on, "But that isn't the only strange happening. One night, I heard The Voice calling my name and I awoke, seeing no one. The Voice said to me, '*You shall know Me for Who I really am*'. I tried to shake myself, but The Voice wouldn't leave me. It's still clear, even now."

"Could it be just your inner mind . . . speaking to you?" Caspian suggested.

Julian shook his head. "No, but I can't figure out what it was. But, that isn't the last mysterious thing." He then went on to tell him the story of Julia's miraculous rescue.

Caspian studied his plate. "How can such things be real?"

Julian shook his head. "Not even I can understand them. I don't see how such things can happen without . . . ." He couldn't find words to speak.

"Well, if their god is real," Caspian shook his head. "I believe it's a strange god."

# CHAPTER SEVENTEEN

## *The Weight of Chains*

Julian and Caspian sat together on the veranda, serenaded by strumming guitars and other instruments that Julian's servants played for them. The stars above them seemed to twinkle, despite the content of their grisly conversation.

"When you capture the Christians," Julian told Caspian, "be certain not to let the soldiers place Lavenya or her daughter in chains. I have been given permission by the centurion to have them brought directly here. Can you see to it that they're safe?"

Caspian nodded. "I will bring them to you myself." Caspian let out a long sigh, causing Julian to turn toward him as he spoke, "I know how much a woman and her child can mean to a man. Remember, I told you about my wife's death."

"Yes."

"Well, I've found a lady in the city I want to marry."

"Good for you." Julian took a long drink as he eyed his beaming friend. "So you found one willing to tolerate you, is that it?" They shared a laugh.

"That's quite right. She's a beauty with long, curly hair. She has status in Rome. We're to marry in a few weeks. My house is waiting for a lady's touch too.

"Well," Caspian said, standing with a grunt, "It's been a fine night, Julian, but the soldiers and I are to leave early in the morning. A soldier needs his rest."

Julian chuckled as he stood, motioning for the musicians to stop with a wave of his hand. "I understand." Julian grasped his hand with a hearty shake. "I wish you and your soldiers safe travel, Caspian. The roads are dangerous."

"In the Roman army, we have the best escort possible," Caspian assured him.

"Good-bye, then." Julian gave him a friendly pat on his back.

"You're a loyal man, Julian," Caspian praised him. "You ought to join the army. We could use men like you to support the legion."

"I'm not what I seem." Julian gave him a weak nod as he started out, escorted by two servants. Julian turned on his heel and called, "Caspian."

"Yes." Caspian turned, placing his hand on his sword.

"You may call me a loyal man." Julian lowered his gaze. "But I'm a coward. If I were loyal, I wouldn't feel as I do."

Caspian studied him. "What do you mean?"

Julian hesitated. "Be sure to instruct the soldiers to deal gently with them." Fabian entered Julian's thoughts as his voice faltered, "They were kind to me."

Caspian studied Julian with a tentative frown. "Be careful where your sympathies lie, Julian. It could cost you your life."

Julian woke before dawn. He washed his face in a water basin. He studied his complexion with disgust as water dripped down his face.

Taking a cloth in his hands, he pressed his face onto the soft material, closing his eyes.

*What have I done?* Julian felt something in him waver. *What have I done?*

Laying the towel aside, he walked onto the veranda, looking at the moon that was still high in the sky. He closed his eyes, feeling a gentle breeze caress his face.

He looked into the distance, past the city walls, squinting. He saw small, glowing torches, looking like small fires in the early morning. He felt something inside of him constrict when he realized it was Caspian and the soldiers, following the directions he'd written.

He watched the caravan of soldiers, seeing only their torches and the swishing tails of the horses. He felt he could hear them, though they were several miles away.

*What have I done? I don't know what is happening to me, or why I feel this way. They were good to me. They treated me so well. Yet, I've rewarded them with their deaths.*

*But if I hadn't have done it, the centurion would have had me killed. I'm not a loyal man. I'm a coward. A terrible, cruel, selfish coward is what I am.*

Lavenya opened her eyes, hearing a small whimper. Thinking of Julia, she sat up hastily and reached for her daughter. She was fast asleep.

Hearing the whimper again, she turned and saw Fabian's frail body, shivering as he sat up. "Fabian?" Lavenya whispered. She hurried toward him, placing a comforting arm around his skinny shoulders. He sniffed away tears as she wiped some of them away with a tender hand.

"What's troubling you?" She gently lifted his chin, seeing his tearful face.

"I had a bad nightmare," he cried. "I dreamed that Joannes died." He sobbed and couldn't speak for some time. "He was killed by soldiers."

Lavenya gently quieted him, fearing he would wake the others. "It was only a dream," she comforted him. "Dreams do not come true. It was only the devil trying to frighten you."

"It was so real, Sissy." He leaned his head against her. "I'm afraid."

"Don't be afraid, dear." Lavenya kissed his forehead. "Take courage."

"Lavenya? Fabian?"

They both turned abruptly and Fabian stopped his crying. Stantius knelt down beside them, wiping a weary hand over his eyes. He studied them with care. "What's the meaning of these tears?" He placed a gentle hand on Fabian's shoulder.

"I had a dream that Joannes was killed," Fabian whimpered.

"Oh, son." Stantius pulled the frail boy into his arms. "Don't think on it any longer. God is watching over Joannes as He is watching over us."

"You must try and get some sleep," Lavenya urged him. "If you want, you can sleep beside Julia and I. Would that make you feel better?" She smiled as he nodded.

Stantius followed them as they lay down. He placed Joannes' blanket over Fabian's trembling body, giving his arm a squeeze. He smiled warmly at them. "I love you both."

Lavenya smiled back at him, feeling such love as he leaned to kiss her forehead.

"I love you too," she and Fabian whispered together.

Lavenya had nearly drifted to sleep when her father sat up in the darkness and said, "Do you hear that?"

Yes, she'd heard it too. "It sounds like someone is outside," she whispered to him and sat up, careful not to wake Julia and Fabian. They heard someone approaching. Lavenya shot a worried look to her father.

Aria came running into the room, crying with dread. She hurried to Lavenya, gripping her hands as she trembled, unable to speak.

"What is it?" Stantius said with dismay.

"The soldiers . . . they . . . just came. They've taken everyone! They're coming . . . here!"

"Oh, no!" Lavenya stifled a scream, causing several others to rouse from their sleep.

"We must flee." Stantius rushed to his wife as she awoke.

*This can't be happening.* Lavenya felt tears rushing to her eyes as she ran to her daughter, yanking her into her arms. *This can't be happening. God, is this really happening?*

Julia began to cry, being roused from her sleep. Lavenya pulled Julia to her chest, waking the others hastily. They all panicked, not knowing what to do.

"We must pray," Stantius urged them.

Lavenya cradled a bewildered Julia to her chest as she wept. She heard horses' hooves and shouts above them. A cascade of rocks came down upon them. Lavenya heard cries and screams as she gripped her daughter to her chest.

Her eyelids drifted shut as she slowly slipped from consciousness.

Caspian entered the darkened room, seeing a group of huddled Christians. He ordered the soldiers to place the Christians in chains. Seeing a thin, older man being chained, he hurried to him. "Which of these are Lavenya and Julia? Have no fear—they're being taken to safety."

The man's kind eyes faltered. "My daughter has fainted. That's my granddaughter."

Caspian looked in the direction where the man pointed, seeing a thin woman slumped over a small, crying girl. He knelt down and turned the woman on her side.

*I can see why Julian found her so pleasing,* he thought, seeing her beautiful features. The child in her arms cried as she clung to Lavenya. Caspian turned his gaze away from the child's pained face as they hauled the others from the room.

The man he'd spoken to was the last to be taken out. The man turned toward Caspian in tears as Caspian leaned over Lavenya and Julia.

"Lavenya!" the man cried as he was dragged out.

# CHAPTER EIGHTEEN

## *My Garment of Tears*

Lavenya felt someone standing over her, placing a cool towel to her forehead. She felt something strangely soft beneath her. Groaning, she opened her eyes, trying to clear her vision.

A woman with long, golden hair was leaning over her.

Lavenya pushed the woman's hand away and bolted forward with a terrified scream. *Where am I . . . and who are you?*

The woman took a step backward. She ran from the room, murmuring fretful apologies.

Lavenya pushed her hair from her face, looking around her in terror.

She was lying in a large bed, surrounded by pillars. The room was finely decorated with sculptures and art work. There were large windows in the room, and underneath them were fine, Roman couches and toiletries. Visions of her own home slipped into her memory.

*What is this place? Where is Julia? Where is everyone?* Her head ached as her thoughts troubled her. She scooted back against the wall, pulling the blankets up to her mouth. She trembled, looking out the large window at a chirping morning bird.

She stifled a cry as a man stepped into the doorway. His silhouette cast a long shadow on the carpet. He was dressed in elegant, Roman garments. Seeing him step forward in the light, she felt her heart break. It was Joannes.

"Where are we?" Lavenya felt tears slip down her cheeks.

"We're in Rome." He walked toward her. "And we're safe."

"Joannes . . . what have *you* done?" Realization finally entered her mind. "It was true! You . . . you are a traitor!" Lavenya jumped up.

He rushed forward, gripping her forearms. "I had to obey the centurion of the army—he would have killed me!"

"You lied to me! *You* . . . lied to me!" Lavenya couldn't speak as she wept, trying to push herself away from him. He gripped her so she couldn't pull away.

*Surely this can't be true! Lawrence was right. He is a traitor!*

"Get away from me!" She managed to push him away and jump from the bed, taking several steps away from him.

"What have you done to my daughter?" she demanded.

"She's safe." He stared up at her with kindness that she knew now was deceptive. "She's in the care of the servants."

"You're lying to me!" she accused. Her eyes were blinded by tears.

Lavenya darted from the room, running into a large hallway. She heard him calling her as she ran blindly through the large house. She slipped on a rug in a large parlor and fell, sliding across the floor. She felt several people help her struggle to her feet.

Julian hurried down the hall after her, seeing that she'd wandered into the main hall.

*What have I done?* Julian watched Lavenya slip from consciousness as she fell into the arms of the servants. They looked to him in desperation.

"Take her to the terrace for a rest in the open sunshine. Then get Julia bathed and dressed and have a meal prepared for them," Julian instructed as they carried Lavenya out.

"Papa!"

Julian spun on his heel. Julia ran down the hall toward him, dressed in a lovely, blue gown. The servants had fixed her hair in a Roman-styled braid.

"You look lovely, my sweetheart—just as you ought to look." He pulled her into his arms, kissing her forehead.

Julia giggled, looking down at her dress. "Pretty!" She threw her arms around him. "Where is Mama? Why did that man bring us here?" she asked.

Julian avoided her question with his hasty answer, "Because you and your mother are to live here with me in my house." Her face glowed as he went on, "Now, would you like to see your mother?" She nodded as he said, "She's lying on the terrace."

"Mama!" Julia squirmed from his arms. Julian ordered a servant who stood beside them to take her to Lavenya. Julian watched her skip down the hallway.

*This is just what I dreamed—Julia's happiness*, Julian thought. *I just hope Lavenya will realize the good in what I've done and find her happiness in my love.*

Julian waited beside the doors that led to the terrace as he listened to them.

"Mama, Papa says we're going to live here with him!" Julia giggled excitedly.

"Yes, he has." Lavenya didn't sound pleased.

Julian turned as the servants walked past him, carrying trays of food. He heard Julia's excited squeal at the sight of the trays of food that the servants set down before them.

"I hope it is to your satisfaction." Julian walked onto the terrace.

Lavenya pulled Julia closer to her, causing Julia to drop the food she held. Lavenya eyed him with a distained look.

"Mama?" Julia let out a questioning cry.

Julian felt his heart stiffen as he sat down across from them, placidly taking a piece of fruit from the tray. He placed it in his mouth, chewing slowly. He took another piece of fruit before he addressed his servant, "Silvia, please take Julia into the house. I must speak with my wife alone."

He saw Lavenya's eyes narrow at his address to her as '*my wife*'.

"Yes, sir." The woman took Julia from Lavenya's arms.

The silence seemed to drone onward as a servant poured Julian a glass of wine. He took a long drink, knowing she was studying him with moody eyes. When their tense gazes finally locked, he saw tears springing into her eyes.

"Why have you done this?" she asked. "Where is my family?"

He ignored her fired questions. "Have a bite to eat, Lavenya."

"How can I eat? I thought you loved me," she said. "You lied to me!"

"I do love you," he told her.

"You don't love me." She scowled at him. "The only person you love is yourself."

He lowered his gaze. "Please, listen."

"Why should I?"

He dipped his bread into a buttered bowl of herbs. "You need to understand me."

"I understand that you lied to me, that you care nothing for God; therefore, you care nothing for me or my daughter, Joannes." She turned away from him. Julian watched the sunlight sparkle on her tears, causing them to look like jewels, slipping down her face.

"My name is not Joannes." She frowned toward him as he murmured slowly, "I'm Julian Galagus—Stephen's brother."

She looked at him with pain in her eyes. "*You're Stephen's brother?*"

"Yes." He nodded gravely. "I was heartbroken when I learned of my brother's death. Mother passed not long after he died—she had a heart attack. It was caused by her grief."

"Because of that, you took your revenge and decided to kill us?" she asked in disbelief.

"If he hadn't joined your sect, he would still be alive." Julian looked up, knowing there were tears in his eyes. "Christianity is a lie to deceive the innocent."

"How can you say that?" Lavenya shook her head, squeezing her eyes tightly shut. "Jesus is the Savior of the world and you have witnessed His power. Still, you will not believe. Your hate has blinded you."

"I cannot believe, Lavenya."

"So you take us as slaves and kill Christians over your unbelief?"

Julian ignored her, turning away to look over the city. He took a grape from a fruit platter, and threw it into his mouth, smashing it with his teeth in anger. "You will live here in this house. You are my wife—"

"Don't remind me." She fumed, turning away from him.

Julian went on with his jaw tightened, "Which means you are to obey me. I am your husband—you must do what I tell you. I am looking out for your protection," Julian persisted. "Not only for your protection, but for Julia's safety as well."

"I cannot be protected in the walls of a pagan house."

He ignored her. "You will be taken care of by my best servants and you will have anything you wish for. You will have all you desire."

"I desire to serve God freely," she said steadfastly.

"I've also arranged that." She turned toward him sharply and waited quietly. Julian pulled out a long scrol from his pocket.

"I paid a high price for this Certificate of Sacrifice for you and Julia. I bribed it from a guard at the palace of Sacrificial Commission."

"And you think bribing is honest?"

"You may worship your god as you choose. As long as you and Julia have this, you'll be protected. Having this Certificate of Sacrifice is the emperor's only demand."

"How can I do that when my family is captured in Roman prisons at the Colosseum? How can I worship and pray in this pagan home you've placed me in? How can I serve God when I know of the others who are dying for our faith?"

"This is the only way you can survive." Julian felt his throat tighten as he choked out the words, "I've done what I can for you."

Lavenya shook her head stubbornly. "You wouldn't have brought me here if you had."

*I thought she would be grateful,* he grumbled in his thoughts. *Instead, she scorns me for trying to save her life. Am I wasting my time trying to save this woman?*

"I've purchased some garments for you. You can change when you are ready," Julian said. "The servants will prepare a heated bath for you."

Lavenya watched through eyes of contempt as Julian walked inside. She felt as if someone had gripped her very soul, and torn it to shreds. The man she loved had betrayed her. Her family was in prison. And she felt alone.

*And he wants me to wear the garments of those who are killing us?* Lavenya placed her face in her hands as she cried. *All I can wear is my garment of tears.*

# CHAPTER NINETEEN

## *Too Powerful a Message*

"**J**oannes is to blame for this." Lawrence crept through the dark cell, sitting beside his wife. He listened to the sound of dripping, hoping it was water. They listened to soldiers march on the street beyond the prison walls.

"He really was a traitor?" Fabian wiped his face, smearing mud on his cheeks.

"Who else could have done this?"

"I'm afraid you're right, my son." Stantius' haggard figure limped toward them. He sank down onto the muddy stone beside his wife and the other families. "Despite our situation, at least we can be assured Lavenya and Julia are safe."

"As far as we know," Lawrence gritted through his teeth.

"God is still on the throne, Lawrence," Stantius said in a scolding voice. "Don't question His plan. He knows what He is doing in our lives . . . and theirs."

They listened to the harsh sting of a whip and a violent scream from another cell. Turning, Lawrence saw a young man being whipped by a soldier. He was held securely in a wooden stock. Fabian shivered under Lawrence's hand.

Hearing the wooden trapdoor above the stairway give a haunting squeak, they turned to see several soldiers walk down into the room. They tossed bits of bread at the Christians.

Lawrence watched the piece of bread a soldier tossed him fly through the air and land in the mud at his feet. Fabian lunged for it and placed it into his mouth, immediately spitting it back out at its awful taste. He choked, placing a hand to his chest.

"Which of you is Stantius?" a stout soldier called to them, stepping forward. Lawrence shot his father a warning look.

Stantius cleared his throat, standing to his feet. "I am."

"Father, no!" Lawrence jumped forward, but Antony held him back.

The soldier walked toward him, handing him a large sack. He placed it in Stantius' hands. "I bring fruit and bread for you from a friend."

"Joannes?" Stantius earnestly gripped the soldier's hand. "How are Lavenya and Julia? Are they alive? Are they safe?"

The soldier backed away from him, releasing himself from Stantius' grimy hands. He straightened with a nod. "I bring you word from Julian Galagus, who you called 'Joannes'."

Stantius' eyes widened in disbelief. "Joannes is Stephen's brother?"

The soldier didn't respond to his question. "They're safe in the home of Julian and are being taken care of by his servants. I assure you that they are protected."

Stantius looked into the soldier's eyes as he cried. "Please give these to my daughter." He handed Caspian several scrolls and looked to him with eyes of compassion. "Also, please send Joan . . . Julian my thanks."

*"For ye have not received the spirit of bondage again to fear; but ye have received the Spirit of adoption, whereby we cry, Abba, Father,"* Lavenya read the words aloud with such joy that she could hardly contain her tears of happiness.

*"The Spirit itself beareth witness with our spirit, that we are the children of God:*

*"And if children, then heirs; heirs of God, and joint-heirs with Christ; if so be that we suffer with him, that we may be also glorified together.*

*"For I reckon that the sufferings of this present time are not worthy to be compared with the glory which shall be revealed in us."*

"What are you reading?"

She jumped at hearing the female voice and stood up quickly from her large bed. It was the same woman she'd seen when she awoke to find herself in Julian's house.

Lavenya mustered a nervous smile as she wiped her tears.

"The Apostle Paul's writings to our people. My father sent them to me. He and my family are in prison." Lavenya eyed her uncertainly as she placed the scroll away. "Where is Julia?"

"She was tired, so the servants placed her down for a nap, Mistress." The servant took a step forward, eyeing the scroll. "Who was the Apostle Paul? Was he the man who was beheaded?"

"Yes, he was a very dedicated man to Jesus Christ. Jesus is God's Son who came and died for our sins." Lavenya smiled at her. "Have you heard of Jesus?"

"Only from the soldiers I've passed in the streets, Mistress. They say people are being martyred in the arena for their belief in that dead man." She lowered her voice, "I've also heard some of the Christians are cannibals."

Lavenya shook her head hastily. "Rumors are rampant, but one thing I can assure you that is true is that Jesus is not dead. He was raised to life."

Silvia frowned. "How can someone be raised to life after they are dead?"

"With God's power, anything can happen."

"Pardon me, but I don't understand that nonsense, Mistress. The master of this house isn't accustomed to this belief."

"He knows about God," Lavenya assured her. "He is just too stubborn to believe; so he has my daughter and I captured and taken like prisoners."

"I'm sorry, Mistress."

"You may call me Lavenya."

"I'm sorry, Mistress, I mean, Lavenya." She smiled. "My name is Silvia." She curtsied to her. "Forgive me for saying this, but your beliefs are strange." Then she frowned as Lavenya wiped her tears. "You're crying?"

"There is much for me to cry about," Lavenya replied. "Some are tears of pain and others are tears of joy. I can't express my thankfulness for these scrolls. My father risked his life to send these precious scripts to me."

Silvia leaned forward. "May I see them?"

Lavenya nodded, handing them to her. "You can read them as long as you'd like."

"You're right about these people—they're strange, indeed." Caspian laughed, removing his helmet as he followed Julian into the courtyard. "You couldn't imagine how I felt when that old man looked directly at me and told me to thank you. I felt as if he were genuinely thankful. How can he thank you when he knows you turned him in? That is past my understanding!" Caspian sighed with frustration.

Julian cleared his throat. "Now you know how I feel about the matter, Caspian." Julian turned toward him as he sank down onto a comfortable chair. Reaching up, he yanked an apple from a tree, and took a large bite. He chewed in meditation.

"Lavenya will come around to our faith," Caspian assured him, sitting down. "What do you think of us having dinner together? I've wanted you to meet Janis. It would be good for Lavenya to meet my lady, too. Then she can see how nice it can be to live as a Roman woman."

Julian continued to chew before he spoke, "She is a Roman, Caspian. Remember, she once lived a wealthy life in Rome, perhaps, not as abundant as this, but she's had her share of this life. She's been adorned, but she's cast it aside . . . for something I can't quite understand."

"They could meet each other. Janis may be able to make Lavenya see reason. She's quite a persuasive lady, as you'll see."

Julian slouched in his chair. "If you say so. Why don't you come tomorrow afternoon with Janis? I'll have a lavish feast prepared for us—one she won't be able to refuse."

"So you refuse?" Julian folded his arms, glaring at the woman who'd become a stranger to him. Lavenya sat with her arms around her knees in the corner of her room. She still wore her soiled dress and her hair was a mess. And she wouldn't say a word.

"You refuse to come?" Julian asked again at her silence.

"I won't wear those Roman garments, dressing as a pagan. I won't be paraded around as your trophy," Lavenya finally said, staring out the window as she spoke.

"*You're my wife,*" he said with frustration. "You shouldn't act like my servant."

"I've been treated like one."

"I've given you everything you desire," he insisted. "What must I do?"

*I can't deal with this woman; she won't listen!* He felt like giving up.

"I want you to be the man I put my trust in, the man I saved from the river, the one who gave me courage. I want you to be the man I loved."

He hastily turned away from her, stalking across the room with a heavy sigh.

From the great hall, he listened to Caspian's loud chuckle as Janis and Julia sang together at their large table. He longed to be with them, but not without Lavenya. He couldn't imagine life without her. Her harsh words stung, stronger than any pain he'd ever felt.

"I'm sorry I'm not," his words were mumbled as he hurried from the room, knowing she must have been staring at him as he left. *I'm sorry I'm not the person you loved.*

Why he felt so torn inside, he couldn't understand. He had brought himself to this fate. Now, he had to get himself out of it.

"Read me that again!" Julia bounced on Silvia's lap as Silvia tried to hold the scroll still in her hand.

She laughed as she read the verses again, "*And he said unto me, My grace is sufficient for thee: for my strength is made perfect in weakness. Most gladly therefore will I rather glory in my infirmities, that the power of Christ may rest upon me.*

"*Therefore I take pleasure in infirmities, in reproaches, in necessities, in persecutions, in distresses for Christ's sake: for when I am weak, then am I strong.*"

"What an encouraging verse." Lavenya leaned back in her chair with a large smile. "In all my weaknesses, Christ is my strength."

The three of them sat in her room, basking in the breeze that floated through the open window. Silvia continued to read as Julia listened intently.

Lavenya sighed, thinking of her family. They were never far from her thoughts. She wondered how they were and what had happened to them. She prayed for them every day.

*In their weaknesses, Lord,* she prayed, *please be their strength.*

Julian sat on the edge of the veranda, leaning over to listen to Silvia as she read. His thoughts haunted him as he listened to the words she spoke, *"For God hath not given us the spirit of fear; but of power, and of love, and of a sound mind.*

*"Be not thou therefore ashamed of the testimony of our Lord, nor of me his prisoner: but be thou partaker of the afflictions of the gospel according to the power of God."*

He felt something stir within him, just as he had felt all those times before when he lived among the Christians.

*There is something powerful about that,* he thought, *too powerful.*

Julian slipped from his bed, hearing someone walking in the hallway. Placing his over garment around his shoulders, he hurried into the hall in the direction of the footsteps. It sounded as if it they were coming from Julia's room.

Stopping just beyond the doorway, he peered inside, seeing a figure leaning over Julia's bed. A thin hand reached out to stroke her cheek—he saw it was Lavenya. She spoke softly to Julia, but he couldn't understand her words.

He waited patiently until she walked passed, not seeing him. He reached out and caught her by the arm, turning her toward him. She let out a frightened shriek.

"Be quiet," he hissed at her. Seeing it was him, she tried pulling away. "I only want to know what you're doing awake this late at night," he said in a calmer voice.

She stopped squirming, but stood an arm's length from him. "I . . . I was . . ."

"You were running away?"

"I was not," she retorted and fell silent, "I was going to the prison."

"You miss your family?" She didn't reply to his question, so he said quietly, "I understand how you feel, Lavenya."

"No, you don't." She tried to pull away from him.

He tightened his grip and answered calmly, "I know more than you realize."

"If you did, you would know that I do miss them."

"I won't let you go out in the streets alone. It's dangerous," he insisted, holding tightly to her wrist. She took a step back from him and sighed with frustration.

"I'll be fine," she said. "I can protect myself."

"You're not leaving if I have anything to do with it."

"Well, you don't," she hissed.

"You are not leaving this house."

"So I am a prisoner?"

"You're my wife—I am going to protect you. If you go traipsing down there in the prisons, you'll be captured. Is that what you want? You want to be killed?" He opened his mouth to continue, but he was too angry to speak.

"There is a scripture that says, *"Blessed are they which are persecuted for righteousness' sake; for theirs is the kingdom of heaven."*

Julian shook his head with frustration, avoiding her eyes.

"You are not going to kill yourself." He met her gaze, seeing there were tears in her eyes. He tightened his jaw and said quietly, "Go back to sleep."

# CHAPTER TWENTY

## *Faces of Pain*

"Aren't you glad you listened to me, Lavenya?"

Lavenya turned at hearing Silvia's voice. She pulled at the sides of the long, beautiful gown without a smile. "I don't feel God would like me to wear these garments."

"Quiet, now." Silvia began to fix her hair as she sat down. "Just getting into clean clothes is not a sin. I think your god will understand that you can't stay in filthy garments."

Lavenya mustered a wavering sigh. "I can't imagine my family living in those dirty prisons and Julia and I are here in comfort. That is on my conscience day and night."

"Well, you pray to that god of yours. Why don't you pray for Him to help you?"

"I have prayed." Lavenya cast her eyes on her folded hands. "I haven't gotten an answer from Him." Lavenya felt Silvia studying her in the mirror she held in her hand.

"Is your god dead?"

"No." Lavenya closed her eyes in agony. "He's alive. He's speaking to me, but I just don't know how to hear Him."

"It seems to me you hear Him well."

"I say that because He isn't changing this situation fast enough for me." Lavenya looked at Silvia in the mirror—her eyes looked so sincere.

"What would you like to happen?" she asked Lavenya.

"I would like my family to be freed. I would like to be away from this house with Julia."

"And what of Julian?"

"I wish I had never married him." Lavenya regretted her words immediately, seeing the maid's eyes widen in surprise.

"Well, you cannot change that, Lavenya," Silvia told her.

"I know." Lavenya sat up straight as Silvia continued to fix her hair. "I know it isn't right to think such thoughts. I shouldn't have said them. I loved him because of his looks—he was the most handsome man I ever saw. Now, I can't say that I love his character."

"He's always been kind to us," Silvia replied. "I was his mother's servant girl before she died. He was always a respectable son to her."

"But he despises us Christians."

"There are many respectable people who do."

Lavenya ignored her hurtful words as she spoke, "I do feel much better now that I bathed, but my heart still hurts."

"That can be expected."

"Thank you," Lavenya said as Silvia finished her hair. She stood with a sigh, walking to the open window. She listened as Silvia put away the perfumes and oils. Lavenya sat down by the window, looking out at the city.

Hearing a giggle, she leaned toward the ledge—Julia was running around on the lower terrace. She wore a lovely, blue gown that flowed behind her as she ran. Lavenya felt a sting of bitterness when she saw Julian chasing her with a large smile.

"How can he be so fatherly to my daughter?"

"What?"

Lavenya turned, seeing Silvia cleaning around the room. "Nothing." She turned back to watch Julian pull Julia into his arms as she squealed happily. He kissed her delicate cheek and spun her around in his arms. Lavenya turned sharply away from the window.

"Did you ever marry, Silvia?"

"Never. I never found one that suited me."

"That's strange—you're beautiful."

The maid blushed. "Beauty often attracts the cowards, I believe."

"Then why did I marry one?" Lavenya asked.

Silvia laughed. "You're much prettier than I am," she said. "Otherwise, your 'coward' would have chosen me!" Lavenya gave her a weak smile.

"At this moment, I wished he would have. But I shouldn't say such things. God has a plan in this, or He wouldn't have allowed it to happen."

"Yes." Silvia smiled. "I believe He does."

Lavenya felt her heart skip. *She believes in Jesus? Perhaps, You do have a plan in this, Lord!* For the first time in forever it seemed, she couldn't contain her joy.

"Ouch!"

Seeing Julia yank her hand away from the rose bush, Julian hastily set aside his glass. He hurried toward her. "What happened?" He wiped a tear from her face.

"I got a thorn in my finger," she whimpered. "It hurts, Papa."

Julian examined her finger and quickly plucked the thorn out. He wiped away the little droplet of blood and bent to kiss her finger. "Does that make it feel better?"

She shook her head as tears slipped down her cheeks. "No."

He felt his heart squeeze as he hugged her. Her crying softened his heart. "It won't last long. Pain goes away after a little while."

*I love this little girl,* he thought. *I love her as if she were my own child. Stephen must have loved her dearly.*

"Master." Julian turned toward his servant as the skinny man bowed. "A man is here to see you about some business. He's from the market."

"He wants some carpeting?" Julian asked him.

"Yes, sir."

Julian set Julia down with a grunt. "Stay away from the roses, darling," he warned, patting her cheek. "Be a good girl while I take care of some business."

She smiled up at him with rosy cheeks. "Yes, Papa."

Julian followed the servant, stopping in the hall as he peered into an open doorway. He caught his breath. Lavenya was dressed in a long gown, with her hair adorned. She was sitting on a stool by the window, reading a scroll.

He thought he'd never seen a more beautiful sight, but when she turned toward him, her eyes were full of pain. He stepped away from the doorway and followed his servant, trying to forget that look in her eyes.

It was as if she saw the intent of his heart and that Someone else did too.

Julian found Silvia sweeping the parlor. She curtsied to him. "Is there something I may do for you, Master?" she asked.

He examined the floor. "You've swept that area enough, Silvia. It looks wonderful, but don't hurt yourself."

She smiled, lowering her head respectfully. "Thank you."

Julian hesitated, seeing the questioning look in her eyes. "I must ask you something."

"Anything, Master."

"How is Lavenya? Please, tell me with all sincerity."

"She's still grieving for her family, but she clings to her faith. She's a strong woman, but I know she's crumbling inside. She . . ." Silvia faltered, "she wishes her god would take care of the situation she's in. She wants her family to be freed."

"I can't free her family," he said with frustration.

Silvia went on, "She prays often at night. I hear her crying, but when I ask her if she's all right, she always says she is. She cries out to her god."

Julian thought over her words. "Has she been eating?"

"Very little." Julian's heart crumbled at her words. "She's terribly thin."

"I've noticed that myself." He then spoke his thoughts, "Silvia, I don't know what to do."

"She longs to know how her family is," Silvia told him.

Julian thanked her with a nod. "I'll send a friend of mine there to see about them—he's a soldier. You may tell Lavenya, yourself."

Caspian crept in the darkness, searching for the man he'd spoken to. He stepped over several bodies lying on the muddy floor, wondering if they were dead or alive. He placed a hand to his nose as a horrible stench filled the prison.

He found Stantius asleep as he was chained to a stake, lying beside several prisoners. His face was thin and his clothes were much more ragged than what he'd seen before.

Caspian shook him. "Stantius!"

The man came awake with a grunt. Caspian then saw that one of the man's eyes was swollen and dried blood was caked at the side of his mouth.

"I'm a friend," Caspian told him. "I bring you food from your daughter."

"And a message?" Stantius' voice strained as he sat up.

"They're doing well." Caspian studied him as he looked through the bundle of food. "I am to report news back to them," Caspian said as the man examined the food.

He didn't speak for some time, but looked to Caspian with painful eyes. Tears slipped down his worn cheeks as natural as if he'd blinked sleep from his eyes. "I don't know if I'd like you to tell my daughter anything," Stantius said weakly.

"But I must. I order you to tell me of your condition. You must understand that your daughter urgently wants to know how you and your family are."

Stantius only shook his head, too choked to reply.

Caspian waited with a frustrated sigh. Then he watched with a curious frown as Stantius handed the sack of food to a thin boy lying beside him. The boy's eyes lighted with pleasure, but only for a few seconds.

"Is this your relative?" Caspian asked.

"This is my son, Fabian," Stantius spoke with a strangled voice. "He's the last of them left." Stantius placed a weak hand on the boy's shoulder with painful eyes.

Caspian frowned. "What do you mean?"

"The rest of my family was killed. Fabian and I alone are left."

# CHAPTER TWENTY-ONE

*"I am Strong"*

*How am I to tell her this?* Julian placed a hand to his throbbing forehead. *They have all died and Stantius and Fabian are the only ones left? How can she bear this?*

"Thank you for your report, Caspian." Julian turned away from him, indicating that he was dismissed. Julian walked onto the veranda, sitting beside a large fountain. Leaning over the water, he saw his reflection in the ripples.

*I knew those people*, he thought, wondering why he felt such sympathy. *I performed my duty to Rome, but I don't feel a bit loyal to my heart.*

He watched a droplet of water land in the fountain, and realized it was his own tear. He sat up quickly, wiping several more with a firm hand.

He looked up, seeing a servant approach him. "Dinner is served, Master."

Julian placed a hand to his stomach. "I'm not hungry," he then turned back to the servant. "I'm retiring early tonight. In fact—" Julian took the servant by his bony arm. "Have someone send the food to the prison. I want it given to the guards with strict orders to have it brought to a man named Stanitus and his son, Fabian."

"Yes, Master." The servant nimbly bowed and hurried away.

Once in the seclusion of his room, Julian let his tears fall freely.

He listened to Julia's soft laughter from beyond his door. Hearing her footsteps on the marble floor, he knew she was running down the hall. He squeezed his eyes tightly shut, wiping his face with a towel.

Sinking down onto his bed, he placed his face in his hands. He hated the war that raged within his heart. For the first time in his life—he wished he were dead.

*I should have been the one who died,* he thought. *Stephen should have lived.*

Silvia hurried up the stairwell, out of breath. With light footsteps, she hastened down the hall and pulled open the door to Lavenya's room. She closed it ever so gently, seeing Lavenya was reading to Julia by a lighted candle.

Silvia listened to Lavenya's gentle voice as she read, ". . . *Whom we preach, warning every man, and teaching every man in all wisdom; that we may present every man perfect in Christ Jesus.*

*"Whereunto I also labor, striving according to his working—"*

"Lavenya," Silvia whispered as she hurried across the room, kneeling beside them, "Forgive me, but I must speak with you." She saw Lavenya's worried frown.

"What's wrong?" Julia asked, grabbing Silvia's hand.

"What is it, Silvia?" Lavenya placed the scroll aside.

Silvia shifted her eyes to Julia and smiled sweetly. "Julia, why don't you leave your mother and I for a while? I'll bring you a treat from the kitchen if you'll hurry and change into your night clothes."

Julia squealed happily as she jumped to her feet. "Yes, I will!"

Silvia groped to catch her breath. Lavenya tried to calm her nervous friend. Silvia finally turned to her with tearful eyes.

"This news is painful for me to tell you, Lavenya." Silvia shook her head painfully. "You have become a dear friend to me since you've been here and you've changed my life."

Lavenya smiled warmly. "God alone changes hearts."

"But you have helped me find Him." Silvia closed her eyes.

"I just spoke with one of the servants who were cleaning the kitchen. Word is spreading around the house that Julian sent Caspian to the prison yesterday with food."

Lavenya leaned forward earnestly. "And are they safe?"

Silvia hesitated, causing a sharp pain to enter Lavenya's heart. *No,* she thought. *Surely it can't be true that . . . they're dead?* She felt tears leap into her eyes.

"They were killed," Silvia choked out the words. "Your father and your brother are the only ones still alive."

"*No!*" the word escaped from Lavenya's lips in a hoarse whisper. She fell back against the bed as tears filled her eyes. Silvia placed a consoling hand to hers.

The faces of her mother and brother slipped into her pained memory. She felt her heart had been crushed with such grief that she could not endure.

*No!* she thought. *No, God! No! This cannot be true!*

Lavenya mourned into the night, unable to sleep. She drifted in and out of consciousness, weeping. Silvia remained at her side, bringing her water and reading her the scrolls, which gave her strength. Lavenya turned over, opening her teary eyes.

In a blurred vision, she listened to Silvia as she read, "*And to know the love of Christ, which passeth knowledge, that ye might be filled with all the fulness of God.*

"*Now unto him that is able to do exceeding abundantly above all that we ask or think, according to the power that worketh in us,*

"*Unto him be glory in the church by Christ Jesus throughout all ages, world without end. Amen.*" Silvia turned toward Lavenya in amazement and said, "That is a great promise."

Hearing Silvia finish reading, Lavenya whispered through cracked lips, "*Amen.*"

"I heard about your family." Julian watched Lavenya weep beneath her pillows. He knelt beside the bed, placing a hand on her cold cheek. She opened her eyes and when she saw him, she pulled away. Julian's heart ached when he saw the contempt in her eyes.

Her eyes were red and her face was tear-stained and swollen from the restless night she'd spent. He knew she'd been crying for several hours, seeing her soaked pillows.

"I'm so sorry," Julian told her, feeling tears spring up in his eyes.

"You're sorry? You led them to this!" Lavenya accused.

Julian felt a wave of guilt. "I know. I'm not sorry for them; they have their reward. I'm sorry for you, but mostly . . . I'm sorry for myself."

Lavenya sat up, pulling her knees to her chest as she wrapped her arms around her legs, leaning her face on her knees.

Julian stood and took a seat in a comfortable chair across the room from her. Looking to the window, he mustered a wavering sigh. "I'm a cowardice man; you don't have to tell me that. There's a war inside me that I cannot seem to overcome. Part of me belongs to my emperor and another part of me belongs to my heart." He turned toward her with tearful eyes. "I don't want to betray either."

Lavenya lifted her head toward him. "You've already betrayed me," she told him coldly. "You have yet to betray your emperor."

"I thought it was the right thing to do," he defended himself. "I acted with you and Julia's safety in mind. I thought this would satisfy you."

"Satisfaction is not what I'm looking for," Lavenya replied. "I'm looking for eternal life. The gods of Rome give me nothing, only death. I have found that the only way to live is in the safety of Jesus Christ. There is no safety outside of Him."

"All my life I've been searching," he said, revealing his inner heart to her. "All my life I've wanted to find a better destiny, something of worth."

"You're looking in the wrong places," Lavenya replied. "You can't find something of worth here. All of these things you have here will vanish—God is eternal."

Julian touched his jaw in mediation as he listened to her words. He shook his head in admiration. "You're a courageous woman, to be so strong. How do you do it?"

"At this moment, I don't feel strong. I feel as if I've been broken into a thousand pieces."

140

"I wish I could help you," Julian said softly.

"What?" Lavenya asked him.

Julian met her gaze with regretful eyes. "Nothing." He stood to his feet and began to walk from the room. He paused as he reached the doorway, turning to meet her gaze. "I love you, Lavenya."

"Do you love God as much as you love me?" she asked him hopefully.

He let out a sigh. "Something tells me that I still don't know Him well enough to answer that question."

Julian remembered the words he'd heard from The Unseen Voice as he walked down the long corridor, *"You shall know Me for Who I really am."*

Lavenya hastily dressed, quietly moving around the room to gather what little she owned. She turned as the door opened.

Silvia walked in, carrying a candle aloft. She frowned, seeing Lavenya gather her things. "What are you doing at this hour of the night?"

"I'm going to the prison."

"You can't—they'll capture you." Silvia caught her by the arm, turning Lavenya to face her. "You can't go. They'll kill you just as they did the others."

"I don't care."

"No!" Silvia insisted in desperation. "You can't leave Julia behind."

"You must protect her for me." Lavenya felt her eyes fill with tears. "I want to see my father and brother; they need my comfort. I need to be with them."

"What must I tell Julian?" Silvia demanded of her.

"Tell him what I've done. . . tomorrow. He can do nothing to save me once I've renounced the gods." Lavenya placed several more things in her bag.

"Aren't you frightened of what may happen to you?"

Lavenya hesitated at her question. "There are a many things I fear, but I know God Almighty—He is greater than all my fears."

"Yes, so do I." Silvia's words caused Lavenya's heart to leap. She went on in a wavering voice, "Thank you for all you've done for me. I will see to it that Julia will always be protected. Will you go see her before you leave, to tell her good-bye?"

Lavenya couldn't speak for a moment. "I couldn't bear that. I'd rather she not know."

"What must I tell her?"

"Tell her that I've left to see about the family," Lavenya decided and tried to speak. Her throat felt dry. "Please take care of her. Follow God and keep His commandments."

"I will," Silvia promised.

Lavenya gulped away her tears. "Teach Julia of our faith. Show her my love."

"Yes. I'll strengthen my own faith in Jesus Christ, as well," Silvia said through tears. They embraced and wept.

"Will I ever see you again?" Silvia asked.

Lavenya smiled warmly at her friend. "Yes, you most certainly will."

Walking through the darkened streets, Lavenya saw sights she had long forgotten. Large, Roman villas and lavish temples for the worship of Roman deities surrounded the city. She gazed up at the moon as it was still high in the starlit sky.

Looking around the city, she saw the Colosseum, rising hauntingly above the landscape. Positioning her bag on her shoulder, she headed toward it. The gruesome sight seemed to pierce her heart. It was the very place where most of her family had died—where she would die.

*Where I will be crowned,* she thought with joyful bounds. *Kings and nobles are crowned in castles, but the martyrs are crowned in the arena. We are honored with a great host, not of this world, but a host of thousands of angels from heaven.*

All of her fears seemed to melt away as she felt renewed strength. It would be a long walk to the Colosseum. Gathering her strength, she began to walk faster.

Before she knew it, she was running.

*I will press forward with all my strength.* She quoted a verse in which she found so much comfort, *"Therefore, I take pleasure in infirmities, in reproaches, in necessities, in persecutions, in distresses for Christ's sake; for when I am weak, then am I strong"*

She smiled through her tears as she ran. *"When I am weak, then I am strong!"*

# CHAPTER TWENTY-TWO

## A Genuine Woman

Lavenya staggered back as she collided into someone. She let out a small cry, feeling strong arms pull her to her feet.

"Where're you headed . . . so fast?" It was a man's voice.

Clearing her thoughts, Lavenya stared into the sleepy eyes of a soldier. "I'm going to the arena," she told him, trying to push past him. The soldier tried to hold onto her, but lost his grip. He staggered after her as she ran and called out shameless remarks.

Lavenya heard someone running after her. She began to run faster, tightening her grip on her bag so tightly that she felt her fingers turning numb.

"Halt in the name of Rome!" another soldier called after her.

She obeyed and turned, nearly colliding with another solider. His forehead wrinkled into a curious frown as he studied her in the moonlight. He gently touched her chin. She pulled away from him.

"What's a beauty like you running the streets of Rome? Don't you know it's unsafe?"

"I'm a Christian . . . and I'm going to see my family in the prison."

The man's eyes widened. He chuckled with blackened teeth.

"Don't you know hundreds of Christians are being killed? Why are you so unafraid?"

"Will you arrest me?" Lavenya asked, seemingly in a pleading voice.

The man lowered his brow and studied her. "You Christians

are a strange lot. Very well—if it's your desire to die, I'll take you there. You could spend the night in our camp—we'd like to have a lady around. I could save your life." The man gave a cruel chuckle.

Lavenya snubbed him. "I'm a married, Christian woman."

Her saucy tone caused him to raise his eyebrows at her. He took her by the arm, leading her to his horse. "I'll take you to the prison. But listen—you won't live more than a few weeks. The Romans are too busy to keep one prisoner very long." He led her to his horse.

A faint whisper escaped her lips, "I will live forever."

Lavenya let out a small cry as the soldier pushed her roughly into a darkened prison. Standing to her feet, she held her bag close to her side and searched the room. Several prisoners were staring at her. She searched for her father and Fabian.

Children were huddled together, sleeping in the muddy hay that seeped into the ground. They looked so nimble and lifeless that Lavenya wondered if they were even alive. It pained her. She turned away, thinking of Julia.

The clanging shackles rang out an eerie song. She heard coughs and mumbles, saw restless mothers, and searched worried faces. There was a stench of death and human tragedy everywhere. Lavenya felt saddened as she looked from face to face. She wondered which child had lost a mother; which father had lost a wife.

*God, you must comfort these people,* she prayed. *We must stay strong, despite these conditions. I trust in You. These people must not give up hope, though they all look so weary.*

Lavenya knew they were suffering, not only from hunger, but poison and other cruel acts by which they'd been abused, all for the sake of Christ. *Let us bring glory to Your name, Lord,* she prayed. *Please give these people comfort and love.*

As she walked slowly through the prison, with the shackles on her legs, her father and brother were at the forefront of her mind. *Where are they?*

She sat down in the muck as the large trapdoor swung open. A soldier peeked into the room. Seeing the door close with a squeak, she got on her knees, straining to see in the dim light.

She reached the furthest wall of the prison, feeling exhausted from crawling. She sank against the stone wall between the back of a feeble man and a woman who slept.

Closing her eyes, she prayed. She listened closely as she heard someone softly singing—it was the thin man beside her.

He began to sing deep and melodiously, sounding much stronger than his frail body looked. In the darkness, Lavenya saw his weathered face that was scarred and bruised. He had a whelp beneath his eye and there was a gash on his lip. She continued to listen to his soft voice as it grew louder. He turned to her with a warm smile.

"Father!" Lavenya threw her arms around him, before he could respond.

He stopped singing and caressed her hair with a gentle hand.

"Lavenya? My daughter, is it you?" Feeling his body tremble within her arms, she knew he was weeping.

She gripped him tightly, never wanting to let go. "Yes!" she whispered joyfully through her tears. "It's me!"

"My daughter!" he cried aloud, arousing the others. Lavenya laughed amid her tears and embraced him. Pulling back from him, she studied his gaunt face. The tears he shed had mixed with the blood on his lip, sending drops of red tears onto his clothes.

He smiled and kissed her forehead. "Please don't look at me with eyes of pain. At this moment, I am free of all my pain." He gave her hand a squeeze. He leaned over and placed a hand on the heel of a boy who slept close beside him. The boy awoke and Lavenya smiled, realizing it was Fabian. She lovingly embraced him.

"Sissy!" Fabian cried. "Where is Julia?"

"She's safe." Lavenya touched his cold cheek. "Through God's grace, I converted one of Julian's maids named Silvia. She promised to keep Julia in good care. I know from how much Julian loves Julia that he wouldn't allow anything to happen to her."

"Does he know you're here?" Stantius asked.

"No, I left without saying anything."

Stantius shook his head. "You're a brave woman."

"I would risk anything to be with you and Fabian, Father."

"Did you kiss Julia before you left?" Stantius asked hopefully. "I hope she isn't afraid."

"I couldn't." Lavenya shook her head. "It would pain both of us too much. I told Silvia to tell her that I left to see about you and Fabian."

"It pains me. I long to see her." Stantius placed a hand to his heart.

"I miss Julia too," Fabian said.

"I brought the scrolls," Lavenya whispered to him and handed him her bag.

They sat for hours, talking to each other of things that had happened in their separation.

"I prefer not to tell you about the others' deaths," Stantius replied to her question. "Sometimes, it is better not to know."

"Did you get the food I sent?"

"Yes."

"You don't look like you've eaten any of it," Lavenya accused.

"That's because I gave it all away." Stantius' eyes lightened as he spoke, "I find it a blessing to keep the children fed."

"The soldiers haven't fed you?"

Stantius let out a chuckle as he leaned his weary back against the wall. "They give us a small piece of bread twice a day and an apple, if they have enough after they're finished. We get all the water we want, but no doubt it's overrun with disease."

Lavenya hugged him, not wanting her father to dwell on their situation. "I'm so glad to see you, Father."

"I'm glad to see you. You're still beautiful and in good health, as I hoped you would be. And you're still serving God." Tears slipped down his cheeks once more as they embraced.

"Papa, where is Mama?" Julia ran up to Julian as he ate his morning meal.

He chuckled and pulled her into his arms, pushing a grape into her mouth. She chewed contentedly. "What do you mean? She always eats in her own chambers."

"She isn't in there," Julia told him as she ate another grape.

"Maybe she decided to eat on the upper terrace. You know how she loves the view from up there."

She shook her head in dismay. "I looked there."

"She may be bathing; you can see about her later. Right now, you ought to eat some of this! I can't possibly eat all this food," he said with a chuckle. She grabbed a handful of nuts that were resting on his plate. She placed them in her mouth with a toothy grin. As Julian watched her, he thought on her words.

"You stay here." He kissed her forehead and placed her in his large chair. "I'm going to see about your mother. I'll be back."

Julian searched the house, unable to find her. He stopped in the hall, seeing Silvia scrubbing the floor with a soiled rag. She wrung it out and pushed the bucket to a different spot to wash, pulling her long hair back from her face.

"Silvia, have you seen Lavenya? I've searched all the living quarters. Is she playing a game of some sort—trying to hide from me?" He folded his arms with frustration.

She hesitated as she stopped scrubbing the marble floor. Turning toward him, her eyes were red from tears. She wiped her nose on the back of her sleeve.

"Silvia?" He knelt down beside her. "What's wrong?"

"I cannot say," she mumbled the words as she hastily shook her head.

"I order you to," he said urgently. "Where is she?" His mind reeled.

She grabbed up her towel, placing it into the bucket of soapy water. She looked at him with distress. "She left." Julian's heart thumped rapidly. "She left Julia in my care . . . and told me she's going to see about her family."

"She turned herself into the guards, didn't she?" he asked her knowingly.

She nodded slowly. "I tried to dissuade her, but she would hear none of it. She was so headstrong about it—I couldn't argue with her. I'm worried she'll be killed."

Julian sank back, leaning against the wall and letting his long legs stretch out in front of him. He turned his gaze away from her, folding his hands in meditation. *So, it has come to this. She's . . .*

*she's going to give up her life for her faith. That's what she always wanted.*

"She'll die in that prison," he said in agony.

"I told her they would kill her, but she was determined."

"Now, I can't help her escape." Julian closed his eyes, feeling his heart constrict, shaking him to the core. *My wife is going to be killed*—the thought devastated him.

"Somehow, I think she believes to die . . . would be an escape," Silvia said, speaking her thoughts. She looked to him with reluctant eyes, afraid to speak.

"You're right in what you've said." He tightened his lips. "Being with God is more important to her than being with me." Sensing Silvia's thoughts through her silence, he turned toward her. "You believe in God, don't you, Silvia?"

"I find it hard to oppose . . . when I see a woman of faith so genuine as Lavenya."

Julian nodded. "So do I," he whispered under his breath.

# CHAPTER TWENTY-THREE

## Change of Heart

Julian sat with his face in his hands. His head ached with grief. Closing his eyes, he cried, thankful no one was around to see him.

*Lavenya is in prison—she will die there. Why is it that I feel I am the one in prison?* he thought to himself. *She has chosen her own death, but I cannot choose . . . because I am a coward.*

Folding his hands in front of him, he gripped them tightly. *Why should I hold onto the belief in our Roman gods? Because Father believed in them? What would I gain to give my heart and soul to our gods? What is this place called "Heaven"? And how can I get there?*

His heart trembled as he whispered, "I want to be saved, God. Please save me."

*I feel You are real,* he prayed. *I feel You are watching me, but that is beyond my understanding. Are You really real?* He looked to the ceiling, searching for a hidden image in the artistry above him. He asked the undirected question—*Are You real?*

He waited. And he thought he heard a Voice. It wasn't audible, but as clear as if someone were standing beside him in the room.

*"The feeling you have in your heart is just as real as I am."*

Julian felt his hands tremble as he closed his eyes tightly and wept. "Yes," he cried. "I finally know You, God! *You are real!*"

He felt such joy, unlike he had ever known. He had found what he'd been longing for.

Lavenya placed her arm around Fabian, reading aloud the scrolls she'd brought. Other children began to gather around them. They were engrossed in the words they heard. Lavenya felt her spirit lighten as she read to them.

They all jumped as the trapdoor opened with squeaking hinges. The children turned hastily, backing toward her in fear. She gripped Fabian, placing the scroll behind her back. Stantius took her hand. They watched soldiers walk into the room.

The Christians seemed to let out relieved sighs, seeing they came with water pitchers and loaves of bread. Lavenya slid her bag behind her father as she took a piece of bread a soldier handed her. The soldier walked past Lavenya, studying her with a grin.

Fabian leaned toward her and hissed, "If that man looks at you again, I'm gonna—"

"Quiet," she hissed at him, yanking on his arm.

Everyone remained quiet until the soldiers left. Hearing the wooden trapdoor close shut, they all began to talk again, quietly at first, but gradually grew louder.

Stantius led the Christians in prayer as they spent that next hour in silent devotion.

Lavenya clasped her brother's scrawny hand as she prayed aloud, "Lord, give us all the strength to face what we must. Allow us to continue in the faith. You are our strength and our deliverer. We trust that You will see us through. You're our fortress. You're our hiding place."

Inwardly, she prayed, *Please protect Julia and give Silvia wisdom to take care of her and teach her. Also, please touch Julian's heart. I know somewhere past his selfishness, he has a heart for You. Please show him You are real, just as You have shown me.*

After her prayer, she pulled a small scroll from her bag—it was the poem she had written. She read it over again and gained encouragement from the words God had given her.

*I know You will send grace*, she thought. *You are my strength. When I am weak, You will be strong for me. I am weak now, Lord*, she prayed. *But in Your power and might, I know I can endure.* She smiled at the thought. *We can endure to the end.*

"Get up!"

152

Lavenya's eyelids fluttered open as she felt someone yank her to her feet. She came awake with a startled shriek as she realized she was being dragged across the room by a soldier. Stantius reached for her with a startled cry.

"Father!" she called to him frantically, realizing there was nothing he could do. *This is it,* she thought. *I'm being taken into the arena to be killed.*

She turned and saw Fabian running toward her. He grabbed her arm, but the soldier gave him a swift kick. Pain gripped Lavenya's heart as she watched Fabian stagger back into the mud, hitting his head against a large stone behind him.

The soldier pushed her up the stairway and pulled down the trapdoor.

Lavenya found herself inside a guarded hall, surrounded by gates. The soldier sat her down against a wall. Lavenya looked around in confusion. The soldier walked through the gate, toward a lighted fire. There were soldiers sitting around their cooking fire.

She moved her legs to a different position, so the tight shackles wouldn't seem so painful. She waited for several minutes as her mind whirled with what they would do to her. Seeing the soldiers turn and gawk in her direction, she grew more and more uneasy.

She looked up, seeing the soldier return with a man at his side. She studied the man's garments, looking up to his handsome face.

*Julian.*

He took a bag of money from his pocket and handed it to the soldier. Julian knelt down beside her as the soldier started away. His warm eyes were compassionate as he took her hand. Lavenya felt too nervous to take it away.

"Silvia told me you came here," he whispered to her, pushing a loose hair away from her sweating temple. "Why did you leave without a word?"

"I knew you would forbid me."

"You're right—I would have." Julian shook his head at her and asked gently, "Why?"

When their gazes met, Lavenya thought she had never seen his eyes more loving, more sensitive. He gently touched her chin.

"You frightened me, Lavenya."

She ignored him with a question of her own, "Is Julia well?"

"She's been asking the servants where you are. She's in good hands though," he said, at seeing her distress. "Silvia is taking care of her." He smiled gently. "What about you? Are you well?"

"My mind is well and my faith is strong—stronger than ever before." As soon as Lavenya spoke, she saw her words troubled him.

He shifted his gaze to their clasped hands. "Do you know you'll die here?" he asked. "You don't seem to realize what you've done to yourself."

She smiled at his words. "I know I'm going to be with God—that is more important to me than this foolish life."

Lavenya did something she didn't anticipate. She gave his hand a gentle squeeze, much like she had done so many times before. "Julian, you can put aside this life. We all must die, but not all of us have a promise of eternity with Jesus Christ.

"This is a hard road, but if God is with you, you have nothing to fear. Jesus promised that He would send us a Comforter—the power of the Holy Spirit," she said.

Lavenya studied his handsome face as he cast his eyes downward. She lowered her voice as she said, "They're killing many Christians. I don't expect to live much longer."

It pained her to see his eyes fill with tears. He hastily wiped them away.

"If you remember nothing else, remember this—some people live to die and others die to live. You must decide. I've made my choice."

"I can't imagine a life without you, Lavenya."

She gingerly touched his coarse cheek. "You don't have to imagine it. If you give your life to the Lord, we will all rise again. You must decide your own destiny." She went on with a smile, "I have no fear of losing my life. Once I rid myself of this temporal body, I will receive a crown of life."

"You seem to look forward to that," Julian whispered.

She smiled. "I do—our sufferings cannot compare to the glory we will see."

He lifted her hand to his lips. "I'd like you to forgive me . . . for doing this to you. I was wrong to try to dissuade you from your faith. I should have known I couldn't."

She smiled as tears slipped down her cheeks. "I forgive you."

"I also want to thank you."

"Thank me? What have I done?" she asked in disbelief.

"You've showed me the way to my faith."

"You believe?" she asked in a joyful whisper. "You believe in Jesus?"

"I have, long before this." He grinned and his eyes sparkled, revealing the hidden truth he'd keep within. "I've been so stubborn . . . but God has spoken to me."

She laughed softly, throwing her arms around him. "Oh, Julian!" She leaned back to look into his eyes. Her heart leapt as he kissed her tenderly. She felt warmth as she had never felt before. He pulled back from her, knowing the soldiers were watching them. She embraced him tightly, never wanting to let him go. "I love you," she whispered as she cried.

"I love you too," he told her.

Lavenya laughed softly, pulling back from him. She blinked away her tears. "I've never been so happy, Julian."

"Neither have I."

Julian released her as the guard approached them. Suddenly, all the joy Lavenya felt, turned to dread. She gripped his hands tightly.

He searched her eyes. "I must go. The guard told me I couldn't stay long." He reached into his cloak. "I want you to have this." He placed a wooden cross in her hands.

"This is the cross you found in that little church?" she whispered in disbelief.

"Yes," he said. "I found it in my bag, but I didn't put it there. God must have been trying to get my attention through some miraculous way."

She smiled and whispered to him, "I'm glad He did."

Julian turned to look over his shoulder at the guard. "Lavenya, I must go."

"Will you come back to see me?" Lavenya asked him hopefully.

"I'll try, my love."

"Julian, please," she pleaded as she cried. She embraced him tightly. "Come see me."

"You will see me again . . . I promise," he whispered, and kissed her good-bye.

Julian walked through the doors of the veranda, feeling a strange renewed feeling in his heart. He watched the descending sunlight, looking toward the arena as it glistened, knowing Lavenya was there. He blinked away tears. Kneeling, he clasped his hands.

"God," he prayed, "forgive me of my many sins. Please, give me strength. Forgive me, for being so hardhearted. I've been a fool not to believe in You. I have witnessed Your power, not only in the miracles You've done, but because You've changed my heart."

"Julian?"

He turned, seeing Caspian being led by his servant. Caspian studied him with a curious frown. He knelt down beside him, seeing tears in Julian's eyes. "Have you gone mad? Talking to yourself?" He chuckled.

Julian looked into his friend's eyes, knowing his face was glowing. Caspian's chuckle faded. "I just came back from the prison after talking to Lavenya," Julian told him.

"And . . . so?" Caspian shrugged. "What happened to put you in such a state?"

Julian gripped his forearms. "Caspian, I believe."

"Julian, do you know what you're saying?"

"Yes." Julian chuckled with vigor. "God is real! He spoke to me! *He is real!*"

# CHAPTER TWENTY-FOUR

## *Captured By Night*

"Lavenya, I was just told there is going to be another execution today." Fabian huddled against his sister, wiping mud from his face.

She took his hand. "How do you know?"

"A prisoner who was sitting by the gate, told me. The executioner told him. Do you think they'll take Father and I?" Fabian gripped her hand as he trembled.

Lavenya placed a hand to her heart. "God will give us strength if we call on His name. You know how to pray, Fabian," Lavenya encouraged him. He nodded vigorously and clasped his hands.

He began to pray, "Jesus, protect Father and I, if we are to be killed today. Please protect Lavenya too. Protect Julia, wherever she is."

"Yes, Lord, please protect all of us," Lavenya continued the prayer. "We believe in You, Lord." She leaned and kissed his forehead as he continued his prayer in silence. Turning to her father, she was glad to see that he slept soundly.

"I'm going to speak to that executioner." She whispered to Fabian, "Stay here."

Lavenya crawled across the muddy floor, unable to stand on her own with the shackles gripping her ankles. She passed several corridors, where Christians were sleeping and talking in low voices among themselves. She reached the gate hall, which led to the arena.

Turning toward the bright ray of light that filled the hall, she looked down the hall, seeing it ended at a large, iron gate, where the executioner was sleeping. She shivered.

There was a stake lying across his chest.

She peered past him into the arena, knowing so many had died there. She crawled toward him carefully, listening to his soft snore.

The closer she scooted to the gate, she more she saw of the arena. Rows and rows of seats towered above the bottom of the arena, which was lined with sand. People began to take their seats, causing her to believe Fabian spoke the truth. She trembled, staring at freshly lain piles of wood that was stacked around the arena.

The man awoke with a start and reached out, grabbing her by her forearms. She let out a startled cry, seeing his menacing eyes narrow on her.

"What is the meaning of this?" he bellowed and pushed her away. "You want to get in there? Well, you'll have your chance soon enough."

"Is there going to be an execution today?" she asked in a wavering voice.

His eyes looked threateningly wicked as he chuckled. He drove his stake into the sand beside him, and gripped it with a closed hand. "This stake has stirred up many a fire around the crosses, where you Christians have been burned." He studied it before turning to her with an impious laugh. "And today . . . it will stir up yours."

Lavenya shook her father's shoulder. He came awake with a grunt. She gripped his sweaty palm. "Father, we're going to be taken into the arena today."

"How do you know?" he asked.

"I just spoke to the executioner." Lavenya placed her arms around his shoulders in a shaky embrace. "They say we're going to be burned on crosses."

"Oh, God." Stantius trembled. "Our testing time has come."

Fabian placed a hand on Lavenya's arm. She pulled him into their embrace as they wept, holding each other for comfort.

"Do not fear." Stantius kissed them. "We will see Christ."

The trapdoor banged open, seeming to shake Lavenya's heart. She held tightly to Fabian and her father as soldiers marched toward them. She listened to frightened screams as the soldiers began yanking Christians to their feet.

Lavenya felt terror grip her as a soldier roughly grabbed her and Fabian. She turned with a distressed cry, seeing her father being forcefully pushed into the grip of soldiers. She listened to the shouts above them.

*Dear God,* she prayed silently as she and the others were pushed forcefully toward the gate hall, *show them Your glory through our death. Please protect my husband and daughter.*

She tried to loose the soldier's grip on her arm, but felt helpless as she and the others were led through the gate hall. The screaming crowd grew louder.

Lavenya listened to the squeak of the iron gate as they were led into the sandy arena. She stumbled, being pushed through the gate. She felt trembling arms help her up, and saw it was her father. Turning to him, she clung to his hand with all her strength.

"Be strong, Lavenya," he whispered to her and gripped Fabian with his other hand.

She gazed around in wonder, seeing thousands of bloodthirsty Romans. The shouts of the hording mob seemed to scream as one voice, throbbing in Lavenya's ears.

She felt a firm hand push her forward and lead her to a wooden cross. Turning, she saw her brother and father also being led to their deaths. Tears dripped down her cheeks.

A soldier secured her arms and feet to the cross, unbearable pain shot through her body. *Oh, God, help me! God, help me!* she prayed, trying to take her mind away from the torture inflicted upon her. She cried out in pain as the soldiers pulled her cross upright.

Hearing Fabian scream, she turned toward him in agony, seeing his frail body being laid on his cross. "Be strong, Fabian!" she screamed to him above the deafening throng.

"Quiet!" a soldier yelled up at her. "This is the end for you!"

Lavenya looked down as the soldiers lit their torches. She lifted her teary gaze to the sky, where the sun shone through the clouds. She felt strength surge within her soul.

"This is not the end," she told the soldier, listening to the roaring crowd. She closed her eyes and smiled, feeling rays of sunlight caress her face. *"This is only the beginning."*

Julian watched Julia play on the veranda, chasing a small puppy that the servants had brought her. She squealed as she ran after the puppy, grabbing for its tail. He chuckled, seeing her pretty gown fly out from behind her.

Turning to gaze over the city skyline, his thoughts turned to Lavenya.

*I'll go see her tomorrow,* he thought. *I'll bring them food.*

He looked toward the Colosseum. Standing to his feet, he walked to the railing of the veranda, looking down at the street, which was crowded with merchants. He thought once again of Lavenya, and looked back toward the arena as his heart pounded.

He heard distant shouts. He stared closer. His throat tightened.

Smoke was rising from the arena.

Julian heard soft mumbling coming from the garden. Stepping from the hall, he found Silvia, kneeling beside a rose bush with her hands clasped on her knees.

"Forgive me for interrupting you," he said gently.

She looked up with a startle and calmed, seeing him. She began to pick more flowers from the bush, arranging them in the vase she had in front of her. She avoided his eyes as she cried. "Yes, Master?"

Julian hesitated. "I'm a Christian now, Silvia."

She jerked her gaze toward him with widened eyes. "You have accepted Jesus?"

"Yes . . . God spoke to me."

"How wonderful!"

"Silvia, if anything happens to me, I want you to take Julia away. I will give you what you need to make a safe passage to a secure province. Don't stay here in Rome. I don't want either of you to be killed."

"I promise I will."

"Good night."

Julian lay awake in bed, thinking of Lavenya. She was always in his mind and his heart. *I can't wait to see her,* he thought.

He frowned, hearing noise downstairs. Thinking it was one of the servants, he turned in the comfort of his bed to find warmth. He couldn't sleep.

His door came open with a vicious slam.

He jumped forward as soldiers rushed into his room. They yanked him from his bed. He was gagged, before he could let out a cry. They began to drag him down the hallway.

One thought burned inside him. *Caspian—he betrayed me.*

He tripped down the stairs, muttering protests as the soldiers yanked him to his feet. One of them said in an intimidating voice, "Keep up, if you want to live another day."

Another of them grabbed a handful of his hair as they pushed him through the hall. "That's what you get, you traitor!"

Fear gripped him as the soldiers began pulling him out the doors of his house. He turned, hoping to get one last glimpse of his servants. He wondered if he'd ever see them again.

Looking to the top of the stairwell, he saw Silvia shivering in fright.

*"Take care of Julia!"* Julian screamed to her, but with the rag in his mouth, his cry could not be heard. Still, he felt a wave of relief as he saw her nod, as if she understood.

Being led by soldiers, he was placed onto the back of a horse and tied securely. He wished he couldn't hear the soldiers' threats as they spoke hatefully to him.

A horseman approached and turned to look at him.

Julian felt his heart sink.

Caspian gave him a wicked smirk. "I told you to be careful of your sympathies—that it could cost you your life. I guess you see now that I'm a man of my word, Julian."

"You didn't keep your word to me!" Julian's words came out in gargled mumbles, causing the soldiers and Caspian to chortle at Julian's distress.

Caspian ordered the soldiers to mount their horses. And they rode off into the darkness.

# CHAPTER TWENTY-FIVE

## Reunited as Brothers

Julian felt blood pour from his hand as it struck a rock beneath him, when he was thrown into a darkened prison beside several other Christians. He gripped his hand in pain, watching Caspian and the other soldiers saunter through the trapdoor above him.

A small boy hurried toward him, wrapping his hand with a piece of cloth.

"Thank you," Julian said, gratefully patting his shoulder.

He peered through the darkness, looking at the many pairs of eyes that were staring at him. Some of them were smiling, others were weeping.

He stood up slowly, walking on the muddy floor, picking up the shackles on his feet. He searched every woman's face for Lavenya. He sat down with his back against a wall.

"Lavenya," he whispered into the darkness.

A middle-aged man who sat beside him, turned with questioning eyes. "Are you looking for someone?"

"My wife, her father, and his son—Lavenya, Stantius, and Fabian."

The man placed a hand on his shoulder. "There were a group of Christians led out yesterday. I believe they were in that group."

Julian turned toward him, remembering when he sat on the veranda, watching the smoke rise from the arena. He blinked, letting the man's words sink into his mind.

Julian's voice trembled as a question slipped from his lips, "Burned?"

He nodded. "I'm sorry, Friend."

Julian placed a hand to his forehead, feeling tears slip down his face. His thoughts troubled him. *Burned? Why so suddenly were they taken from me? I hadn't even the opportunity to tell them good-bye.* He envisioned seeing their bodies burning.

He crumbled to his knees and wept.

After a long while, Julian removed his tear-stained face from his soiled knees, feeling the man touch his arm. The man handed him a small bag. Julian studied it, questioningly.

"This belonged to your wife—she brought it here."

Julian held the bag to his heart, as if it were a rare treasure.

"Thank you." He looked toward the man with appreciative eyes as he left him.

He pulled out several scrolls from the bag and began to read, feeling his spirit lighten.

*Thank You for sending these words to comfort her,* he prayed. *Thank You for comforting them in their time of trial. I know You will also comfort me in my time of testing.*

Silvia began packing with the servants, placing food and garments into two large bags. She let out a haggard breath as she donned her shoes. She hurried to Julia's bed and woke her. Her eyelids fluttered as she smiled in the sunlight.

"Is it morning time?" she asked with a large smile.

"Julia, you must hurry and dress—we're leaving." She watched Julia's little face contort as she frowned and sat up, wiping the sleep from her eyes. She stood with her hair a mess.

"Where are we going? We going to see Mama?" Silvia turned away from her as she placed several more things in their bags, hoping Julia wouldn't see the pain in her eyes. Julia repeated the question, but Silvia acted as if she didn't hear. Instead, she turned to her with a smile and handed her a small gown.

"Where are we going?" Julia repeated.

"We're going on a journey—you and me."

"But what about Mama and Papa?" Julia asked her with a wavering frown.

"We'll see them later," Silvia told her. "But we must leave."

Silvia helped her dress, praying steadily. Walking to the window as another maid helped Julia with her hair, she peered in the street below. The servants were preparing their horse.

Julian held the scroll in his worn hands as he read, *"Blessed be God, even the Father of our Lord Jesus Christ, the Father of mercies, and the God of all comfort;*

*"Who comforteth us in all our tribulation, that we may be able to comfort them which are in any trouble, by the comfort wherewith we ourselves are comforted of God.*

*"For as the sufferings of Christ abound in us, so our consolation also aboundeth by Christ."* Julian wiped away a tear, feeling such love in his soul. It was as if a hand had reached into his heart, taking away his pain.

"They all died in the faith," Julian comforted himself as he continued to read. "They all died for You, Jesus . . . now they have eternal life."

"Amen," Julian heard someone beside him say.

He turned, seeing an elderly man dressed in rags. He was humpbacked with wrinkled hands. His smile seemed vaguely familiar.

"I believe that too, young man," the man told him kindly. "I've felt that too."

"Which of your relatives was taken?" Julian asked him sympathetically.

He shook his head, turning away from him. "Not one by blood, but we are all family here." The man smiled. "We are family through Jesus Christ."

Julian studied the man, seeing his recognizable features. He took in his features with quick scrutiny—*Long nose, grayish hair, square jaw, and brown eyes. I have seen this man before, but where?* Then he remembered where he had seen the man. *This is that strange man that I stole the horse from in the woods!*

"Marcus?"

The man's eyes lighted. "I thought that was you, Julian."

"How did you get here to Rome?" Julian asked, amazed at their reunion.

"Well," Marcus said with a chuckled, "I walked."

165

Julian's smile faded as he lowered his gaze. "I apologize. It was wrong of me to take your horse. I would give it back, but—"

"I have no use for it now," the man interrupted. "But you're forgiven. It appears both our paths have led us here. If my horse led you to Christ, I was glad to help."

"It was a hard journey."

"It's been a hard choice for everyone to make, but it will be worth it when we all see God's face." He smiled, patting Julian's arm. "It'll be worth everything we pay."

"Marcus," Julian said, mustering a sigh, "I want to know God better. I feel as if I still do not know enough about Him."

"We will all witness His glory." Marcus grinned. "I welcome death." He turned with a smile toward Julian. "I guess we are now two of those 'fools'."

Julian chuckled, remembering their conversation on the road. "It appears we were the real fools not to believe in Christ. At least we've come this far."

"We're not at the end," Marcus assured him. "We have only begun our journey."

"How did you get here?"

"I met some Christians on the journey to Rome," he explained and laughed. "Perhaps it was better that I walked. If the Christians would have heard my horse, they would have fled. I went to a stream to wash and stumbled upon some children who were playing in the water. I followed them to a little hideaway, where I met some very courageous Christians.

"I stayed with them until we were reported. We were all brought here. I'm the only one left, but . . . ." Marcus faltered. "I've heard the Colosseum will be open tomorrow. I have no doubts that they'll take me."

"Are you frightened?" Julian asked in hesitation.

"Not at all." Marcus smiled. "I have a hope of my reward. I am clinging to the hope that someone will witnesses my death . . . and be changed forever. I want to be a witness to those who will come after me.

"The Christians who live a hundred years from now will fight the same struggles we do. I must help them decide to follow God, no matter the cost."

Julian felt his heart soar as Marcus spoke. The man's hope and joy seemed to lift his spirit. He shook his head, unable to fathom Marcus' determination. There was a zeal in him, unlike he had ever witnessed before.

"You're giving your life to save others?"

"That is what Jesus did for me . . . and I want to be like Him."

After sitting in silence for some time, Marcus turned to look at the scrolls in Julian's hands. He pointed toward them. "What are you reading?"

"A copy of Paul's letters to the church in Corinth."

"Would you please read them to me?"

"Of course," Julian answered without a question. He felt it would be an honor to read to someone who had the courage he longed for.

He unraveled the scroll and began with some verses, in which he'd found great comfort, *"For God, who commanded the light to shine out of darkness, hath shined in our hearts, to give the light of the knowledge of the glory of God in the face of Jesus Christ.*

*"But we have this treasure in earthen vessels, that the excellency of the power may be of God, and not of us.*

*"We are troubled on every side, yet not distressed; we are perplexed, but not in despair;*

*"Persecuted, but not forsaken; cast down, but not destroyed."*

Marcus nodded with a smile and repeated, *"Persecuted, but not forsaken; cast down, but not destroyed.* Praise the great God of Heaven."

Julian turned toward him, seeing Marcus' eyes were closed. A single tear slipped down his weathered cheek as his lips moved in silent prayer. He felt such tenderness as he'd spoke.

He remembered how Marcus had always addressed him as "Friend". He patted Marcus' shoulder as he finished his prayer. "I'm glad we've met each other again. You have strengthened my faith. I'm thankful I had the opportunity to ask your forgiveness. You called me your 'friend'—now, I hope that can be true."

Julian was taken by surprise as Marcus shook his head slowly. Marcus' eyes then twinkled with a kind smile. "You're not my friend—you're my brother."

# CHAPTER TWENTY-SIX

## *Last Words*

Marcus was taken into the arena the next morning.

Julian spent that night in restless vigil, praying for the ones who had died. They had become his family in such a short time. Joining the other Christians, he shared Lavenya's scrolls with them. They listened to readings in the late hours of the night for comfort.

Julian watched light creeping through the gate hall, knowing dawn was approaching . . . which meant another day of bloodshed.

Julian rubbed at the whelp behind his neck. He wished to stop the pain that crept up his spine, ending in a pounding headache at his temple. He leaned against the stone wall, wishing to break the heavy chains on his wrists. His eyes felt heavy as the afternoon droned on.

Peering through the darkness of the prison, he watched prisoners talk to each other in muted whispers. Some of them had painful tears, others had tears of joy. Across the room, someone was singing—the sound seemed to reflect the very chorus of his heart.

He reached for Lavenya's bag—the only trace of her left with him. He felt tears run down his face as he pulled out the wooden cross.

He held it for a long time, looking at its carvings, remembering when they'd found it. He remembered the feeling he'd felt inside, but now it was stronger. He not only held the cross in his hands, but in his heart.

A small boy crawled toward him, looking at the cross in his hands. "Who are you?" the boy asked him as his eyes darted back to the cross.

"Julian. What's your name?"

"Olivius. Where did you find that cross?" The boy reached for the cross, and Julian let him have it with a kind smile. He put a hand on the boy's shoulder as Olivius studied it.

"I found that cross in an old church. One of our brothers or sisters must have carved it from a piece of wood. The church was destroyed by soldiers."

The boy continued to look at the cross. His eyes glowed.

"You can keep it." Julian felt his voice break as he said, "I can't . . . anymore."

The boy's eyes lighted with pleasure. He studied the cross in disbelief. Julian was about to speak, but stopped himself, seeing the boy's eyes were clouded with tears. Julian was taken aback as the boy hugged him. Pulling away from him, the boy gripped the cross to his chest.

"My father was a preacher," he said. "He died when the Romans burned our church, but I escaped with my mother. This . . . was the cross he carved."

"God meant it to be in your hands." Julian couldn't push aside the joy he felt. "But always remember—it has touched my life."

"Yes, I will . . ." the boy was interrupted by the familiar squeaky hinges of the wooden trapdoor.

Soldiers came rushing into the room.

Julian gripped the boy by his shoulders, turning him away as other Christians were taken. Julian watched their faces as they were placed in chains. They cried, but he knew their tears were not of pain, but of joy. *It is an honor for us all to die*, he thought.

Julian met the eyes of a soldier who walked toward him. His boots sounded deathly harsh against the stone floor. "Get ready— you're next." His words seemed to strike Julian's heart. "You can save yourself if you renounce your god."

Julian didn't respond. The soldier walked away.

The boy's eyes widened as he snapped his gaze toward him. "They're going to kill you next!" His eyes began to water. "I just met you . . . you're my friend!"

Julian placed a consoling arm around his shoulders. "We must all be brave." Julian lowered his voice. "God will give me the courage that I need to overcome this. I have 'kept the faith', just as Paul said. I have finished the course God wanted me to do." The boy trembled as Julian spoke, "Now, you must be brave for those behind you."

"I will pray for you, Julian," the boy replied.

"Olivius, I will also pray for you." Julian embraced him tenderly, remembering how it felt to hold Julia in his arms. He wished he could comfort him. Lavenya's words suddenly returned to him. He pulled back from the boy and gave him a smile. "Just remember—*some people live to die and others die to live.* We are going to die, but we will live forever."

"Yes, we will." The boy nodded. "Good-bye, Julian," he whispered.

He watched the young boy hurry to his mother with the cross in his grip. He showed his mother the cross, and they embraced. Their tears brought happiness to Julian's heart—he knew they were tears of joy. Julian smiled as Olivius' mother kissed him.

He reached into Lavenya's bag as his thoughts raged. *So this is it. I'm going to die for my faith as Lavenya and the others have done before me.* He let out a shaky breath.

He cried as he pulled a scroll from the bag. Opening it, his heart leapt as he found the poem Lavenya had written. He read the words in a whisper,

*"Our garments cast shadows on stone.*
*The weight of our chains causes our hearts to groan.*
*We sigh as we long to be free,*
*Our children cry, but cannot whisper a plea.*

*"We sacrifice ourselves for the opportunity to live,*
*Our blood, we are willing to freely give.*
*We know it will be worthwhile in the end,*
*If we continue, God's grace He will send."*

He gripped his heart, leaning his head on the cold stone behind him. Above him, he heard the shouting throng in the arena. The Christians around him stirred in prayer.

But something inside of Julian was unafraid.

Amid the grimly chorus in the raging arena, he reached for the feather pen and ink well in the bottom of the bag. He closed his eyes gravely.

*Lavenya, you've given me strength,* he thought. *You've led me to this faith. You've helped me understand. You've spilled your blood. You've received your crown. Now, I must receive mine. I will finish this poem for you, my love.*

*Please, Lord, give me strength,* he prayed.

Julian dipped the feather into the ink well. He shuddered, hearing the thunderous roar from the arena, and prayed once more. He struggled to stop his trembling hands. Tears rolled down his face. He wrote—

*I will die for Christ and face the flame.*
*I accept my death amid their terrible game.*
*I know that if I press on, it will not be a loss,*
*For this day, I will be crowned at the cross.*

172

# AUTHOR'S NOTE

This is my first published novel. Though I've written other stories, I've published this first because of its meaning to me. I was so inspired by the life and death of the martyrs and the scriptures I found in the Bible to support the faith they died for. The Bible must have been such an encouragement to them amid their excruciating trials.

I've tried not to paint the executions in a fantastic depiction. This is my view of the persecution. It was more brutal and terrible than anyone has ever imagined, but I also believe that their faith was as greater than anyone has ever imagined. The story of the martyrs has captured me, and I hope this story has touched you as it has blessed me to write it.

*"And what shall I more say? for the time would fail me to tell of Gedeon, and of Barak, and of Samson, and of Jephthae; of David also, and Samuel, and of the prophets:*

*"Who through faith subdued kingdoms, wrought righteousness, obtained promises, stopped the mouths of lions,*

*"Quenched the violence of fire, escaped the edge of the sword, out of weakness were made strong, waxed valiant in fight, turned to flight the armies of the aliens.*

*"Women received their dead raised to life again: and others were torched, not accepting deliverance; that they might obtain a better resurrection."*—Hebrews 11:32-35

Gelina Gilbert

# ABOUT THE AUTHOR

Gelina Gilbert is seventeen and lives with her parents and twin brother in Houston, Texas. Her sister is twenty-three and lives in Austin, Texas. Her cousin (who was raised with her) is nineteen and joined the Air Force in 2008. He is based in Washington State, and lives there with his wife and baby daughter.

She began reading and writing historical fiction at age nine. She soon discovered the joy of writing about Jesus. She has continued in that passion ever since. She's written over eighty poems and loves to write songs. She's written seven novels, six children's books, three volumes of quotes, two short stories, a religious inspirational, a play, and now she's working on her eighth novel. This is her first published novel.

She is very active with her youth group where she attends church in Humble, Texas with her family. She regularly participates with church activities and group sports. She enjoys assisting with Sunday School, the yearly VBS, and interpreting for the deaf. She also has been the assistant at her church library for four years.

Music is also very much a part of her life. She plays the flute and trumpet in her church band. She also plays the 5-string banjo and is now learning the piano. She loves to sing and praise God. Listening to Christian music is one of her favorite pastimes.

As for her future, writing is very much involved in her dreams. She hopes to continue her education in writing when she graduates in 2010. Whatever God plans for her life, she will always continue in the passion that has transformed her—writing about God's goodness and truth.

She uses Habakkuk 2:2 to enlighten her words, *"And the Lord answered me and said, Write the vision, and make it plain upon tables, that he may run that readeth it."*

# CONTACT PAGE

Gelina would love to hear your comments.
You may contact her at:

**Crownedatthecross@yahoo.com**

CPSIA information can be obtained at www.ICGtesting.com
225885LV00002B/6/P

9 780982 558911